Sign up for our newsletter to hear
about new and upcoming releases.

www.ylva-publishing.com

You're Fired?

Shaya Crabtree

Chapter 1

"I REALLY HATE YOU."

"You know you say that to me literally every shift, right?" Phoebe didn't look up from her computer screen. "I'm numb to your anger by now."

Rose glared from across the cubicle. Phoebe ignored her and kept typing until Rose diverted her attention back to her own computer.

"You're the reason I have this stupid job," Rose said.

"I'm the reason you're able to pay your bills and afford your tuition. But whatever helps you sleep at night."

"I could've worked at McDonald's," Rose whispered, laying her head against the desk. "I could be eating a free burger right now."

Phoebe scrunched her nose. "You'd smell like french fries all day."

Rose sighed. "French fries. Hot and sizzling straight out of the fryer and not frozen like this goddamned office." She shivered. "Why do we have a fan on in the middle of winter? It's December!"

"Because this office is like two feet wide and there's a hundred people in it," Phoebe told her. "Turn that fan off and we'll all be sweating. This place will reek of B.O. faster than Garth's gym."

Garth's gym. I should have gotten a job there. Fit, shirtless men. Ripped women walking around in nothing but their underwear. She could get fit and consume eye candy at the same time. That was the dream life. Too bad that Garth was Phoebe's ex. Rose would never side with him after their breakup. Instead, desperate for a part-time job, she had agreed to help Phoebe do data entry for this stupid company in this stupid office. Literally nothing could be more boring, but it paid her college fees and that's what mattered. Only another month of this and she'd have saved up enough to leave work behind for the semester and focus on school.

Rose tugged her cardigan closer around her body. It was entirely unintentional when her hand slipped into her pocket and she pulled out her phone. She was good at letting her personal life distract her at work.

Twenty minutes after descending into Facebook Hell— surprisingly without reprimand from Phoebe   Rose looked up to see her screen had gone black. She moved the mouse frantically, hoping it was just the screen saver, until she gave up and accepted reality. Her computer had shut itself off again, and she was left staring at her reflection in the darkened monitor screen. The harsh lighting in the office made her blonde hair look white. She did like her new lip gloss, though, even if her lips were turned down in a pout. It brought out the brown of her eyes.

"Goddamn it," she yelled, smacking the monitor on its side. "This stupid thing is older than I am. It shuts down every time I leave it idle for too long."

"Why were you leaving it idle?"

"Shut up, Pho."

"Point Phoebe. You know, you could just fix it yourself. Why are you spending all that money on tuition if you're not going to use your degree?"

Rose pressed the power button on her tower. The lights flashed, followed by a whirring that sounded like a lawn mower, and slowly the computer began rebooting itself. Rose sat back in her chair, unlocked her phone, and waited. "I took some computer science classes, not archaeology classes. I know how to fix real computers, not dinosaurs like this one."

"You could figure it out," Phoebe said.

"I could," Rose agreed, "but why put the tech department out of a job? Plus, computers aren't my favorite thing in the world. I'm better with numbers. Unlike whoever decided that broken staplers were a better use of the budget than new computers. Do the rest of Gio's branches operate like this or is it just us? Because I have no idea how any company can be internationally successful yet behind the third world in terms of technology. Where is all this money we're making going?"

"Hey, Rose. Hi, Phoebe." At the sound of her name, Rose looked up to see Mason approaching.

Rose and Phoebe's cubicle was in the back corner, far away from most of the people who did the real work in the office. They seldom had visitors. Rose was glad to see Mason, though.

"Hey! What's up?" she greeted him.

"Oh, nothing much." He rested his arm over the cubicle wall. "I'm just bored and on my break. Have you guys drawn for the Secret Santa yet?"

"We're doing a gift exchange?" she asked, surprised. "I hope someone gets me a new computer. This thing's a piece of shit." She gestured at the monitor which had blacked out again while she talked to Mason. This time she didn't even attempt to turn it back on.

"Need me to fix it?" Mason asked. "I can do it in…" He glanced at his watch. "Ten minutes when I'm on the clock and getting paid for it."

"Sounds good to me." Rose shrugged, then turned to Phoebe. "And that's what I mean by keeping the tech department in business."

He turned to head off, but Phoebe's cry stopped him. "No, wait!" He froze mid-step like a burglar caught sneaking into a house.

Phoebe cleared her throat. "I just mean… You're off the clock. You should get one of the other technicians to do it. Like…Harley. Maybe."

Mason and Rose shared a knowing look, and Mason took a step back.

"All right," he said, grinning. "I can get Harley to come over here

3

for you. I'll get her to bring the Secret Santa bowl too, so you can draw out your names."

Phoebe nodded and returned to work with a satisfied smile. Rose grinned too, then stuck a finger down her throat in a gagging motion for Mason's benefit. He laughed, and Phoebe shot them both a suspicious glare.

Rose feigned innocence. "Hey, don't look at me like that. All I've done today is save Harley's job by giving her work to do. You should be grateful."

"So who'd you draw for the Secret Santa?" Phoebe asked Mason, changing the subject.

"You'll never guess."

"You're right, I probably won't."

There were too many people at this company for Rose to know all of them, especially when she was confined to her cubicle most of the time she was here. Aside from traveling across the office to the bathroom or to the kitchen on breaks, Rose hadn't seen much of the place. If her computer actually worked like it was supposed to, she would never even have met Mason or Harley.

Mason dug into his pocket and held up a piece of paper proudly. Rose squinted to read it, but Mason was all too eager to tell her. "Bailey."

Rose racked her brain for a moment to place the name. "Is Bailey that hot manager you have a crush on?"

"He sure is," Mason confirmed, folding the strip of paper and slipping it back into his khakis. "Drawing his name was the most luck I've ever had."

"Or it was fate," Phoebe offered kindly.

"Fate. Luck. Whatever it is, I'll take it." Mason glanced at his watch again. "Anyway, I better get back to work. I'll make sure to get Harley for you, Pho."

Phoebe blushed but recovered well and offered Mason a small "thanks" before he left.

Rose continued to ignore her computer. She'd care about it again once Harley made it operable. Until then, she had better things to preoccupy herself with.

"So," Rose drawled, wheeling her chair closer to Phoebe. "You and Harley, huh?"

Phoebe pushed her away playfully, sending Rose rolling back to the opposite side of the cubicle. "Whatever, Walsh." Phoebe spoke confidently. "Harley's hot and you know it."

"I didn't say she wasn't," Rose agreed. "You should go for it. I'm just jealous you're moving on from Garth so fast. I haven't been with anyone since Chad, and I'm starting to wonder if I should hit on Harley myself."

Phoebe glared at her. "I saw her first. She's mine."

"Gross, Pho," Rose scolded playfully. "She's not an unmarked plot of land you can stick a flag in and call your own. If that's how you treat women perhaps I should let Harley know."

"Rose, you know I wouldn't—"

"Joking." Rose held her hands up. "You're so snappy today. 'Bout time you got laid again."

"You're one to talk," Phoebe said. "Garth broke up with me two weeks ago. Chad broke up with you two *months* ago. Have you even talked to anyone else yet?"

"Well there was someone who tried to hit on me a few weeks ago," Rose said tentatively. "But I turned them down. Not for the reason you think," she quickly interjected. "Not because of Chad. He was a shitty boyfriend, and I'm over him."

"Someone was flirting with you?" Phoebe asked curiously. "What the hell? Why didn't you tell me? We're best friends. We're supposed to tell each other everything."

Rose shrugged. "I didn't think you'd want to know."

"Of course I want to know!" Phoebe exclaimed. "Who was it?"

"Your brother."

The silence in the cubicle was almost as awkward as it had been for Rose to be hit on by her best friend's brother. Phoebe didn't take long to break it.

"Ew. You're right. I didn't want to know. I think it's safe to say that Christopher has officially hit on everyone now."

"Pretty much."

"For real, though." Phoebe shifted backward. "You should find someone new. Or at least get laid sometime soon."

"I know." Rose sighed. "But I don't trust any random dude to pick me up in a bar for the night, and girls always want to take things further. I don't think I'm ready for another relationship yet. Not while I'm busy with school and work." Rose paused for a moment, considering. "Some sex sure would be nice, though."

"Masturbate more," Phoebe offered helpfully.

"Tried that," Rose answered honestly. "I'm already bored of touching myself."

"Then spice it up."

"Huh?"

"Get yourself a nice dildo."

Rose chewed her bottom lip for a moment. "That's...not a bad idea, actually."

"Of course it's not," Phoebe said. "Have I ever given you bad advice?"

Rose could recall many, many nights when Phoebe had urged her to drink those extra shots. Or to pour more vodka into that Moscow Mule. She recalled the mornings after those many, many nights. Mornings spent on the bathroom floor in front of the toilet. And she could also recall the day Phoebe had suggested Rose take this job.

Before Rose could call Phoebe out on all of the awful advice she had given her over the years, Harley peeked her head around the corner of their cubicle.

"I heard there's a computer that needs fixing?"

In one hand Harley held her tool box. The other gripped a small bowl filled halfway with folded strips of paper, which she set on the counter.

"Yes." Rose rolled away from her desk to give Harley more space to work. "It's a piece of junk. I'm not even sure it's worth fixing at this point. I need a new one."

"No way this office can afford new computers," Harley told her, crawling underneath Rose's desk. "They haven't had a budget for that since the nineties, judging by the age of this thing."

Rose could have figured that out. It was clear from day one that whoever was operating this place either didn't have money or didn't have any idea how to allocate it. If Rose were in charge of an international corporation like Gio, her employees would have a lot more to work with than mediocre equipment and a lack of job security. Hell, if all went according to plan, she could get her degree and buy Gio out in ten years. With Rose in charge, maybe this branch would actually be successful and everyone here would make the wages they deserved.

"Oh, you guys can draw names if you want." Harley gestured to the ceramic bowl.

Phoebe smiled and settled the bowl on her lap. Rose reached between her legs to grab a name.

Vivian Tracey. Rose had never heard of her.

Phoebe busied herself drawing a name, and her eyes went wide as soon as she read the slip. She tilted the paper toward Rose. "Look," she whispered.

Rose read. *Harley Dayton.*

"Fate," she said, and Phoebe nodded.

"You look happy." Harley glanced up from where she was unscrewing the cover of Rose's CPU. "Who'd you get?"

"Wouldn't you like to know?" Phoebe teased. "It's called a Secret Santa for a reason. I'm not telling anyone whose name I drew until the gift exchange. You'll just have to wait to find out."

"Boo." Harley pouted. "Who'd you get, Rose?"

"I have no idea," she said honestly. "Some girl."

Harley nodded understandingly. "Yeah, I have no idea who the person I drew is either. Guess I'll meet them at the Christmas party."

7

Rose watched Phoebe's face brighten at the word *party*. It wasn't the first time. "When's the party?"

"Christmas Eve. We've still got a couple weeks until we have to spend money we don't have on complete strangers we don't care about."

"Do you think someone'll get me a new computer?" Rose asked hopefully.

Harley scoffed. "Yeah, if hell freezes over like this damn office. Have you seen this place's budget? They're in the fucking tank. I can't believe they can even afford to pay us as much as they do, and they sure don't pay us a lot. The insurance here barely covers enough physical therapy for me to pay for the rest on my own. I know we're just regular employees, but even the managers can't make much more than us."

Rose and Phoebe nodded in understanding.

Harley snapped the cover back on the tower. "Well, your computer should work for at least the rest of the day. It's still a piece of shit, though. There are some miracles even I can't perform." She crawled back out.

"Thanks, Harley. You're a life saver."

"Don't mention it." Harley tossed her tools carelessly back in the toolbox. She took much more care in grabbing the bowl off of Phoebe's thighs, standing closer than she needed to.

Rose let them have their moment.

"Well, I guess I'll see both of you at the Christmas party." Harley tucked the bowl against her side.

"You most definitely will," Phoebe said.

Harley's smile widened. "See you around, Pho."

"Damn," Rose said after Harley left. "She totally has a thing for you."

Phoebe leaned back in her chair, throwing her arms over her head and stretching. "I know," she moaned. "And it's so great."

"I'm jealous," Rose admitted. She missed the thrill of infatuation. The breathlessness, the giddiness. The way that special someone made her body feel. The way she could think of no one else. But at least she could live vicariously through her best friend.

"You should be jealous, Rose," Phoebe said dreamily. "You should be very jealous."

"So I ordered two of them."

Rose was actually working for a change and had been for the past couple of hours. Her computer hadn't shut down in days, and it was so refreshing to have the screen stay on that Rose thought she'd take advantage of the opportunity and help out Phoebe by doing some work.

"Two of what?" Phoebe asked distractedly, glancing over from her own desk.

"What you told me to buy," Rose said. "Dildos."

Phoebe paused. "Why do you need two?" Her hands hovered over her keyboard as she focused on Rose. "I'm going to regret asking that, aren't I? Never mind, don't answer. I don't want to hear about your weird double penetration fetish."

"They're not both for me." Rose's face scrunched in discomfort at the thought. "Plus they were on sale. Buy one get one free."

"Who else are you buying dildos for?"

"Whoever this girl I drew for the Secret Santa is."

Phoebe quickly trundled her seat over to Rose and said in a harsh whisper, "Rose, you cannot give some random girl a dildo for Christmas. You are going to get in so much trouble for that."

"What are they going to do? Fire me?" Rose looked Phoebe straight in the eye. "Oh no!" She gasped and clutched her face. "What a *tragedy*."

"Rose, I'm serious," Phoebe whispered. "That's an awful idea, and you know it."

"I think you meant to say a *hilarious* idea," Rose corrected. "And incredibly economical."

"It won't be hilarious if you embarrass that poor girl and she files a sexual harassment lawsuit against you," Phoebe said.

"Come on, Pho. It's just a gag gift—it's not that serious. I'm sure she'll laugh at it. This office is so boring. I can't be the only one dying for a little excitement. You have to admit it is kind of a funny idea."

"Okay," Phoebe said, taking a breath. "It's *kind of* funny. But in the story way. If someone told me they did that once upon a time, I'd laugh. But if my coworker slash best friend is telling me they're going to do it and probably get themselves fired, it's not quite as funny. At least get the girl a real gift, too. One she can actually show her children when she gets home and they ask her what she got."

Rose sighed. "Fine. We'll compromise. That's one of your better ideas, I guess."

"Hey. Have I ever given you a bad ide—"

"Yes," Rose cut her off. "You're giving me party-pooping ideas right now. When I tell this story to all our friends and they laugh their asses off, I'll let them know how you tried to stop me and ruin the fun."

"Bitch."

"Damn right I am," Rose said proudly, opening a browser on her computer. "I guess I'll buy the girl some soaps or a candle or something. You know, in case she wants to use the dildo in the bathtub or have mood lighting while she fucks herself. Or both."

"You're a perv."

Rose ignored her.

"Did you order the dildos online, too?" Phoebe asked. Rose nodded. "You think everything will show up before Christmas Eve?"

"Of course. I even got free delivery."

⇒∘⟨∞⟩∘⇐

The first package arrived right on time.

Right on time for Rose's mother, Beth, to answer the UPS man at the door. Which would have been fine if she hadn't opened the box.

When Rose came home to find the cardboard package with the tape already ripped off its lid, it was almost as traumatizing as that time in seventh grade she came home to find her mom reading her diary.

Rose didn't even take time to look at the box's contents. She marched to the living room where her mother was on the couch watching TV.

"When you told me I got a package in the mail, I didn't think you'd *opened* it." Rose glared at her mother.

"If it's any consolation, I wish I hadn't," Beth said, her gaze faltering as she looked at Rose. She turned her head to look intently at the TV screen instead. "I won't go through your stuff anymore," she promised. Rose didn't believe her. "I didn't know you were expecting anything, and I thought there might have been a mix-up."

"Well, just to warn you before you go on another ransacking rampage like an airport baggage inspector, I have another package coming soon."

Beth winced.

"It's soap!"

Beth shut her eyes and waved her hand dismissively. "I don't want to know, ok? I'm sorry. I'll make sure to leave your mail alone and put it in your room when it arrives."

Rose sighed. Her mother should have done that with this particular package. Who cared if she opened a box to find an innocent bath set? "Thanks," she said half-heartedly, and headed off to her room.

She called Phoebe immediately.

When the call picked up, Rose wasted no time with pleasantries. "Guess what I got in the mail and guess who opened it before I got home?"

"Gross," Phoebe mumbled.

"Yeah," Rose said. "I'm twenty-three. I really need to move out of here. You and I should get an apartment together next semester."

Phoebe scoffed on the other end of the line. "Yeah, right. Christopher could never afford a place on his own. Unless you want to live with my brother and endure him hitting on you 24/7, that probably wouldn't work out. Plus, what would your mom do? You pay most of her bills, and you can't exactly leave her to fend for herself while she doesn't have a job. The guilty conscience would be worse than living with Christopher."

"At least he wouldn't open my packages."

"No, but if he knew you were ordering sex toys, he'd be offering to help you test them out as soon as they arrived. Not worth it."

"Good point."

"I know it is."

"Anyway." Rose braced her phone between her shoulder and her ear, freeing both of her hands to pull back the flaps on the box.

The cardboard was innocent enough on the outside, in that it was free of any information that might give away what the product was or the company who made it. The contents themselves were drowned in packing peanuts, which only showed that Beth had gone to extensive lengths to see what was inside. This only irked Rose more.

It took a solid thirty seconds of digging for her fingers to find both sharp plastic packages the dildos were encased in. When she finally freed them from the box, her eyes went as wide as she imagined her mother's had.

"Holy shit, Pho," she breathed into the phone. "These are way bigger than I thought they'd be."

"Pardon the pun, but can you expand? Are you saying 'holy shit, the size of this thing makes it even more hilarious for the prank,' or 'holy shit, fucking myself with this is going to be epic'?" Phoebe asked.

"Both?"

"Gross."

Moving to sit on the bed, Rose tossed one of the dildos back into the box where it landed with a thunk. She retrieved her phone from her shoulder with her free hand and kept her grip on the second package with the other.

The plastic around the dildo was translucent, giving Rose a

preview of exactly how big and how detailed this thing was. She had severely underestimated the size of eight inches and had severely overestimated the size of all of her ex-boyfriends. The strip of paper in the background of the package showed some shirtless, muscled dude, and Rose was too afraid to read any of the text beside it. The dildo itself was hyper-realistic, more veiny than she thought actual dicks could be and thicker than was probably safe. If it wasn't missing the balls and redder than Phoebe's blush when Harley was around, it'd be a dead ringer for the real thing. A mutant, overgrown version of the real thing, but still.

"I'm so excited about this prank, Pho. You've got to see this thing."

"Send me pictures," Phoebe suggested. "I want to send them to Harley. I was telling her about your prank, by the way, and she loves it. She thinks you're going to get fired, but she also thinks it's going to be hilarious."

"So you and Harley are already at the point where you're discussing sex toys?" Rose asked. "Wow, Phoebe, you move even faster than I thought."

"Shut up."

"I'm kidding. How'd you get her number?"

"She gave it to me," Phoebe said. "I ran into her by the water cooler and we got to talking. Next thing you know, she's putting her number in my phone."

"Harley Dayton doesn't seem like the type to hang out by the water cooler."

"She was *fixing* the water cooler."

"God." Rose sighed. "I thought she only did computers. Is there anything that girl can't fix?"

"Nope." Phoebe boasted. "She's already doing a good job mending my broken heart, too."

Rose laughed. "Wow, that was probably the cheesiest thing I've ever heard anybody say. But I'm happy for you. When's the wedding?"

"We're eloping to Vegas in the spring. You can't come."

"Whatever," Rose scoffed. "I'm going to be right there beside

Elvis in that drive-through chapel when you're saying your vows and feeding Harley that same shitty line about fixing your broken heart that you just told me."

"I wouldn't have it any other way."

"Good."

Rose tossed the dildo into the box with the other one. She was tired of looking at it. The more she stared, the creepier it became. She closed the box and slid it under her bed for the moment. She'd worry about wrapping the gift later when the soaps arrived.

"What'd you get Harley?" Rose asked. Phoebe had been stressing for weeks about finding the perfect gift, and it was nearing the time when she'd have to commit to a decision. There were only so many days left before the party.

"I got her this watch. It's supposed to be scary accurate and waterproof and indestructible and shit. It's got a compass and tells latitude and longitude, whatever that means. I have no idea how to work it, so I'm guessing Harley will like it."

"Sounds perfect to me," Rose told her. "It also sounds expensive."

"Yeah, well, when your Secret Santa is probably going to be your next girlfriend, you shouldn't be afraid to go all out."

Rose nodded. "I almost spent more on my gift than I should have," she said. "But I did get that deal, so it was worth it."

"Definitely. Good thing you're good with money, because you certainly won't be making any after you get fired for this stupid prank."

Rose rolled her eyes. "See, you keep stressing that point, but I still don't care. Getting fired doesn't sound that bad. This job sucks."

Phoebe sighed, defeated. "And it's gonna suck a lot more without my best friend there to keep me company."

"You could always quit."

"Yeah, right," Phoebe scoffed. "Some of us don't have our budget planned out so well that we only have to work part of the year."

"Sucks for you."

"Go fuck yourself."

Rose glanced to the edge of her bed where she knew the box was tucked out of sight. "I might."

"Ugh." Phoebe gagged. "I didn't need to hear that. And you suck. I hope that girl's soap doesn't arrive in time and you're stuck wasting your money on it and giving her only the dildo."

"Yeah, right. Like that'll happen."

———⧫———

Phoebe Connor was a god.

Or at least had good connections with a couple of demons. Or maybe oracles? Rose's second package did not arrive in time for the party.

Telling Phoebe she was godlike was not Rose's proudest moment. Nor was admitting she was wrong. That was harder than wrapping a dildo in gift paper without the shape of the thing immediately giving away what it was. Rose ended up having to wrap the package in its box.

"I can't believe you didn't get her a replacement gift." Phoebe shook her head in astonishment.

"What was I supposed to do?" Rose asked. "Give her the half-used bar of soap I washed my ass with this morning?"

"I think it's funnier that it's just the dildo," Harley said.

"I think it's irresponsible," Phoebe said.

As honored as Rose was to witness their first squabble as an unofficial couple, a bigger part of her wanted to get to the party before it was too late. "Stop fighting and let's go get food. I don't want to arrive when the refreshments table has been picked clean. You know how much Mason loves snack cakes."

The acquisition of free food was something neither Harley nor Phoebe wished to delay. They called a truce and followed Rose across the office.

The break room was decorated for the holidays as cheaply as possible. A small felt Christmas tree sagged in the corner by the coffee pot. A string of red and green lights was draped over the top of the door frame, and someone had gone through the effort of hand-crafting a string of identical paper snowflakes only to snip them apart from one another and tape them individually to the backs of the windows. It was festive. A little pathetic, but festive.

The room was packed, and Rose's line of sight bored through the crowd of bodies to focus solely on the snack table where Bailey was pouring himself punch. Mason stood beside him stuffing his face with Hostess Christmas Trees.

"Hey, Mason. Hi, Bailey."

"Rose!" Mason quickly covered his mouth and swallowed before speaking again. "Rose. Look at this cool tie Bailey got me." He grabbed the tie around his neck and showed it to Rose while he spun around slowly like a model. "He was my Secret Santa, too! What are the chances?"

Rose studied the tie carefully, looking for something that set it apart. It was just...blue. A standard, not particularly fashionable tie. Which was strange considering Bailey had the jawline of a Greek god and looked like he belonged on a Milan catwalk. Maybe he knew Mason didn't care as much about fashion as he did. Rose decided to let it go and lie. "Yeah. It looks...great."

Mason leaned closer and whispered, "It's got a flask on the back." He spun the tie around to expose a thin, elongated metal tube. Mason could easily store a few swigs of his famous moonshine in it. With this job, he'd need it. Bailey and Mason winked at Rose in sync.

"Now that is pretty cool," she admitted. "Are we really giving gifts already? I thought someone was supposed to give a speech or something."

"The boss is," Bailey told her with a shrug. "I just got too excited and couldn't resist."

"In that case." Harley handed her present over to Phoebe. "This is for you."

Phoebe looked like, well, a kid at Christmas. "Shut up." She gasped. "You drew my name?"

Harley looked confused until Phoebe handed her own gift over. Harley laughed in disbelief.

"Phoebe Connor, I don't believe it. I shouldn't have taken my eyes off that bowl. I bet you dug through and picked out my name on purpose."

"I'll have you know I picked your name on the first try, thank you very much. You can ask Rose."

"It's true." Rose snatched one of the last few snack cakes before Mason could grab it. She hoped Mason had spiked the punch with his new flask.

"Hey, Bailey?" Rose took a sip from the cup. The red slurry was disappointingly alcohol-free.

"What's up?" he asked.

"You're a manager, right? You know everyone here?"

"Pretty much."

"Can you show me who Vivian Tracey is? I drew her name and I have no idea what she looks like."

"Oh, sure." He stood on his tiptoes for a moment and looked around before pointing to a woman hovering near the front of the room. "She's over there. Curly brown hair. Cute gray blazer. Kinda tallish. It looks like she's talking to Jana."

Rose spotted her immediately. "You're a saint, Bailey."

"No problem."

The crowd was denser now, and navigating through was harder than the first time. Especially with a drink in her hand. Vivian was hard to lose sight of, though. Rose had seen her swanning around but didn't know what department she worked for.

Up close, Vivian was intimidating. She was not much older than Rose. Her eyes were a piercing green, and her hair was layered in a stylish cut with auburn highlights. Her tailored blazer and matching skirt graced an athletic figure and told Rose this woman put as much thought into her work appearance as Bailey did. She looked beautiful, crisp, and professional.

She also looked like the type who would rat Rose out after she found out what her gift was. Rose figured it was best not to linger in her presence for very long. She adjusted her plan. No hanging around for a hearty laugh together. Approach, hand over the present, say "Happy holidays," and back away. She'd be gone before Vivian could remember her face.

By now Vivian and Jana were watching her dithering on their periphery. They looked curious yet impatient, as if she had interrupted an important conversation. It was too late to back out now.

"Hi. I'm your Secret Santa," Rose said, putting on her best fake smile. She held out her gift.

Vivian took the package tentatively and shot Rose her own polite smile. "Thank you."

"Happy holidays." Rose retreated rapidly.

"You too," Vivian said, before turning back to her conversation and letting Rose slip away.

Mission accomplished. Rose quickly made her way back to her friends.

"What did you get Vivian?" Bailey asked when she returned.

Rose was still riding the high of her own joke. "I probably shouldn't tell you this since you're technically one of my higher-ups," she said. "But I trust you. Get this." She laughed. "I got her an even better gag gift than you got Mason. I gave her a dildo."

The color drained from Bailey's face. Mason looked pale, too.

"Please tell me you're joking," Bailey said in a hushed voice.

"Nope."

"Rose," Mason whispered, "Vivian Tracey is the president of this entire company."

Rose looked to Mason, then to Bailey, waiting for one of them to burst into laughter and tell her they had teamed up to prank her. Neither of them delivered the punchline.

Rose tapped Phoebe on the shoulder. "Does Vivian Tracey really run this company?"

"Yeah. Why?"

Rose swallowed. Hard. "I just hand-delivered a dildo to her."

Phoebe's eyes bugged out of her head. "You drew *Vivian's* name?"

Rose nodded.

Harley patted her on the shoulder. "It was nice knowing you."

"I have to get that present back." Rose began to head for the front of the room when an authoritarian voice rang out. It was Vivian's.

"Hey, everyone!"

"Too late." Mason grabbed her. "She's started her holiday speech."

Rose froze. She had until Vivian finished her speech to figure out if she was going for fight or flight.

"I know this year hasn't been easy and we've seen more than a few of our friends and coworkers lose their jobs," Vivian told the hushed room. "But I say we take a moment to be thankful this holiday season that we're still here. The company has scraped through another year and that's all thanks to you guys."

"Run," Harley told Rose. "You've got two good legs. Use 'em. Slip out of here while no one's looking. Go type up your letter of resignation at your desk, collect your shit, and get out. Vivian will kill you if she catches you."

"Vivian's going to kill everyone if she opens that box," Phoebe said. "We're never going to have a Christmas party again. Go get your stupid gift back from her!"

In the face of such contradictory advice Rose had to admit running sounded better. Saving *herself* sounded better. But—always a but—she couldn't let the rest of her office go down with her. Phoebe was right. If Vivian found out any of Rose's friends knew what she was up to and didn't stop her, they would all be out of their jobs. She had to get that package back.

She pushed her way through the crowd just as Vivian was finishing up.

"You all deserve a little break. So go ahead and have fun. Eat the food, exchange your gifts, and enjoy each other's company. I'll see you all back in the office after the party." Vivian raised her cup in toast.

Halfway across the room, Rose saw Vivian tearing open the gift wrap. She cursed under her breath, sped up and stomped on more than a few toes trying to maneuver her way through the crowd faster.

By the time she'd squeezed through the lid was off the box and Vivian's hand was firmly gripping something in the middle of the sea of packing peanuts. The pupils of her eyes grew wide enough to be mistaken for eight balls.

It was too late. Far, far too late.

"What'd you get?" Rose overheard Jana ask.

Before Vivian could respond, Rose burst in between them. "It's just a gag gift. I left the real present at home this morning by accident. Silly me." Rose slapped her forehead to underline her stupidity. "I'm such a mess."

Jana eyed Rose suspiciously, obviously trying to place her. Vivian eyed her, obviously trying to decide what to do with her dead body after she killed her.

Rose tried her best to smooth over the situation. "You know what?" she continued to lie. "I think I'll go home on my lunch break, get the real present, and then bring it to your office later. How does that sound?"

The snake-like speed at which Vivian replaced the scowl on her face with a wide, wicked smile scared Rose even more than her earlier death glare.

"Yes," Vivian said sweetly. "I would *love* to see you in my office later."

Rose swallowed hard and tried her best to keep her cool.

It didn't work.

Chapter 2

ROSE ALWAYS THOUGHT SHE'D GO out with a bang. She'd party as hardy as possible until it was time to face the consequences of her actions. In this case, meeting Vivian in her office that afternoon to arrange her own funeral. Except the office party wasn't where she wanted to chew off the foot she'd already put in her mouth. It was far preferable not to be in the same room as Vivian when she didn't have to be. Instead, she went back to her desk and contemplated her demise.

She could still run, as Harley had wisely suggested. She could slip out of the office while everyone was at the party, go home, wait for the angry phone call—the one she wouldn't answer—delete the voicemail message telling her she'd lost her job, and just not show up at the office ever again. It could be that simple. The Risk Analysis class she took last semester would advise her to run and minimize her chances of paying the consequences. Of course, it would also remind her that she couldn't afford it. Her wallet was banking on the exact amount of time she'd need to work with Gio to come up with her funds for the rest of the semester. There were still twenty-eight days left on the clock. One hundred working hours. Four more weeks. She'd be skipping out on a crucial chunk of change.

Rose opened and closed a few desk drawers. She didn't really have anything to pack. The most personal thing she kept at her desk was a pack of gum; she stuffed stick after stick into her mouth until the package was empty and tossed it, along with the wad of wrappers, into the trash can in the corner.

Now there was nothing to show she had ever been here. No evidence to leave behind.

They could keep their shitty computer, the spinning chair, the drawer full of office supplies she now contemplated pocketing. She'd given the boss a dildo, so a pad or two of sticky notes seemed like a fair trade, right?

Phoebe's side of the cubicle was much more personal. Her purse sat by her chair. There was a framed picture of her and Christopher on the desk. And a Post-it note with Garth's name, a heart around it, and then a big, angry, red X on top of that, stuck to the wall. Phoebe cared about this job. She had settled in and become comfortable. She had something going for her here and if Rose ruined that by dragging Phoebe into this mess or leaving her without a partner to help her with work, she'd never forgive herself.

Phoebe was right. She had to face Vivian and take the brunt of the blame by herself. She couldn't let Vivian come looking for her and risk having Phoebe or any of the others be the ones she let her anger out on. Besides, it was cowardly to run.

"You're still alive?" Phoebe came up behind her. "You ran off. Harley and I placed bets on which town park Vivian was going to bury you in." Behind the jokey bravado her eyes were full of worry.

"Put me down for five dollars on 'tosses my body in the dumpster.' I haven't talked to her yet. I mean, I *did*, but only long enough for her to tell me to meet her in her office once the party is over. I think it goes without saying that she opened her present before I got to her."

Phoebe sunk into her chair. "Well, I've got more bad news for you," she said. "Party's over."

Rose groaned. "Thanks, Pho. What would I ever do without you?"

"Probably give your boss two dildos instead of one."

"You're probably right." Rose shook her head. "I should've given her mine, as well. I'm never going to be able to look at it after this, let alone use it. Vivian's more likely to do something with it than I am."

"I don't think she could use both at the same time," Phoebe told her. "She's already got a stick up her ass."

"Well, maybe she can replace it with the dildo. Sounds more sanitary."

"Yeah, I'm sure she's calling you into her office to thank you for helping her hygienically shove things up her ass."

"God, what if she shoves it up *my* ass?"

"That's probably more pleasant than what she's actually going to do to you"

Rose slumped, banging her forehead against her desk for probably the last time ever. It was a poignant moment. Her jaw smacked nervously on her gum. "I'm fucked."

"Again, that would be better than what she's actually going to do to you."

"You're not helping, Phoebe."

"I tried to help you two weeks ago when you told me you were buying a dildo as a Secret Santa gift," Phoebe argued, pulling her chair up to her desk and starting up her computer. "But did you listen to me? No."

"If the party's over, I should probably be making my way to her office now. I'm putting it off, though."

"It shouldn't be too bad," Phoebe reasoned. "The worst she can do is fire you. Well, actually, she could charge you with sexual harassment, and I wouldn't really blame her if she did because she definitely has a case. Though I doubt this company has enough money to handle a lawsuit, so if she does that she'd probably be out of a job too, which I'm sure she doesn't want. I'd imagine the worst that'll happen is that she fires you."

"Yeah, you're right. I saw this coming, so I shouldn't be that afraid." Rose stood up and slid her chair back under her desk. It was now or never. "Better get going before she comes looking for me."

Phoebe nodded, then stood and wrapped her arms around her. "Good luck."

Rose buried her head in Phoebe's shoulder. Her voice came out muffled against the collar of her button-up. "Thanks."

"Don't mention it. You're gonna do fine. But just in case, should I start putting your stuff up on eBay to help pay for the funeral?"

Rose pulled away from Phoebe with a fake glare. "Some friend you are. Speaking of my stuff, I told Vivian I had her real present, but, uh, I don't. The soap didn't come on time. Should I give her something anyway?"

"Wouldn't hurt." Phoebe shrugged. "Probably won't help either, but it's worth a shot."

"God, what do I give her, though?" Rose panicked, searching her desk for something usable. Her hands met metal and she held the tool up in the air. "Think she could use a stapler?"

"That stapler doesn't even work," Phoebe pointed out.

"Of course not." Rose slammed it back down. "All right." She braced herself, hovering in the entryway of the cubicle. "Forget the gift. I've got to go. Make sure I look fabulous at my funeral."

"You got it, girl. Love you."

"Love you, too."

Vivian's office shouldn't have been hard to find, considering it was the nicest room in the building, but it was. After wandering around the maze of the main office Rose found herself by the tech support station asking Mason where to go. He knew exactly where Vivian's office was (apparently not even the president had working equipment), but the whole time he was giving Rose directions there was a sadness in his eyes and a sympathy in his voice that made Rose feel patronized, as if Phoebe had stuck a *dead woman walking* sign to her back when she hugged her good-bye. It didn't help calm her down.

When she found Vivian's office, the first thing she noticed was that the door was surrounded by glass windows. That was good.

Vivian could hardly murder her without someone witnessing it from the outside. The second thing she noticed was that Jana was in Vivian's office with her and they were both poring over a file, their heads almost touching.

She barely had time to sit down outside Vivian's office before Jana came out. She gave Rose a knowing look. Then, smirking, she shook her head and left, calling back over her shoulder, "Nice gift. Wish you had been my Secret Santa."

Rose was left sitting there, speechless, wondering why Vivian had told Jana about the gag gift. If it was such a joke, then why was she here worrying herself sick?

She swallowed her gum and entered the office, shutting the door behind her.

Vivian hadn't moved from behind her desk. She was preoccupied with something on it, and it took her a moment to notice that Rose had come in. When she saw her, her face didn't soften, and given the way she was scowling, that was not a good sign.

Rose swallowed again.

Vivian straightened her jaw. "Sit." She didn't even need to gesture to the chair. Rose slowly sank into the seat in front of Vivian's desk and waited for a trap, like the chair to strap her down and electrocute her. She shifted uncomfortably.

Vivian finally looked up after Rose had stewed for several minutes.

"I must admit, Ms. Walsh," she said. "This *is* the most creative way any of my employees has ever told me to go fuck myself."

Rose didn't expect Vivian to start off with a joke, but she knew better than to assume this was going to be a light-hearted conversation, especially considering Vivian had already figured out her name and who she was sometime in the past hour since the party. She might have been joking around, but she wasn't messing around, and Rose would rather get straight to the point and get this meeting over with as soon as possible.

"Look, I'm really sorry," she said. "It wasn't like that. I honestly did get you a real gift, I just ordered it late and it didn't arrive on time. I had no idea you were the president of the company, and I just wanted to have some fun. The gag idea was stupid and I'm sorry. I won't pull it again."

Vivian smiled wickedly. "No, you won't." Vivian hardened her features. "But believe it or not, I'm glad you pulled this little stunt on me rather than someone else. This is a lawsuit waiting to happen."

"I don't want that," Rose said, knowing she couldn't afford a good lawyer. "I'd rather just be fired."

Vivian toyed with her pen for a moment, clicking the end repeatedly until the tip poked out, then disappeared back into its sheath of plastic. She seemed to be scrutinizing Rose's level of honesty carefully. Rose didn't expect her next words.

"Who said I was going to fire you?"

She scrunched her brow. "Aren't you?"

"I was," Vivian admitted. "But someone suggested I keep you around."

Rose choked on the lump in her throat, and it wasn't the gum climbing its way back up from her stomach, it was emotion.

"Phoebe?" If Phoebe had risked her job to approach Vivian at that party and ask her to go easy, then Rose owed her one. She couldn't ask for a better friend.

"No."

Or a shittier friend.

"Who then?" Had Harley done it? Mason? She was too scared to mention their names.

"Jana. She's the vice president of the company. You're lucky she got to me before you did, or we wouldn't be having this conversation right now. You'd already be out the front door."

"Oh. What does she have to do with this?"

"I was ready to fire you on the spot, but Jana is the one who pulled up your files." Vivian lifted a manila folder from her desk and held it up for Rose to see. "This says you're an Applied Mathematics major. You any good with numbers?"

"That's usually what math entails, yes."

"Ever done any accounting?"

Rose bit back a "more than you" and settled on, "I've dabbled."

"Good. That means you'll do fine with your new assignment."

"New assignment?" Rose asked. "You mean I'm really not getting fired?"

"Not yet," Vivian said. "We need someone to double check a few financial reports for us, and someone with your skills shouldn't be doing data entry. If you can prove yourself useful, I might forgive your little misstep."

This was going much better than Rose had planned. Too well. There had to be a catch. "Let me get this straight. I gave you a dildo, and you gave me a promotion?"

"I wouldn't call it that," Vivian said. "But I am giving you a new office."

"Where is it?"

Vivian pointed to the corner of the room where Rose noticed an open door and an adjacent room so small it didn't deserve the title of office. "That's a storage closet," she said.

"Yep."

"There's not even a desk in there."

"We'll work something out."

"So my punishment is basically a time out?"

Vivian nodded. "Seems fitting, doesn't it? Juvenile stunt, juvenile punishment."

Rose was in no place to argue. "All right. When do I start?"

"Now," Vivian said, rising from her chair. "While you go get your things from your old station, I'll round up that desk for you."

"So we're done here? Just like that?" Rose released her grip on Vivian's desk, which she hadn't even realized she was holding. She also didn't realize how strained her knuckles had been until they ached as they detached. She stretched her hands out by her sides to bring back the blood flow.

"Not quite."

Rose braced herself for more stipulations on her new job, but

Vivian did nothing except pull open a desk drawer and hand Rose a neatly-wrapped package from inside it.

"Your Secret Santa said they couldn't find you at the party. I told them I would give this to you."

Rose took the gift like it was a bomb. The crinkling of the wrapper as the present exchanged hands startled her like the hissing of a fuse. She looked briefly for a tag, searching for something to let her know this was a genuine present and not some counter-prank Vivian had whipped up right before she'd come into the office, but there was none.

It didn't take Rose long to realize she was being paranoid. Vivian thought too highly of herself to sink to Rose's level and start some kind of prank war with her, but Rose wasn't about to ask her boss who the gift was from and confirm it. It didn't really matter who it was from, anyway. It wasn't like Rose would know the person.

"Thanks."

"You're welcome."

A beat passed where Rose stood in front of Vivian awkwardly, waiting to be dismissed or given another set of instructions, but nothing came. Vivian shuffled the papers around on her desk, closing the cover on the front of Rose's file and tucking it away in the cabinet behind her. When she spun back around in her chair, she seemed surprised to see Rose still standing there.

"Do you need something? Would you like your dildo back as well?" Vivian's tone was mocking, and Rose didn't bother humoring her. With a very intentional eye roll, she made her way to the door.

"Try to save the attitude for someone else," Vivian said as she turned the handle.

Rose paused with her hand tight around the brass of the knob. It would be simple to flick her wrist, open the door, and leave without saying a word, but Rose wasn't the type to surrender the last laugh.

"Don't worry, I've got enough of it to go around."

Rose wasn't about to leave her old cubicle without telling Phoebe what had happened.

When she went back to her desk, Phoebe was not the only one waiting for her.

Mason, Bailey, and Harley were there too, all smushed into the cubicle that barely had enough room for two. Mason and Bailey were practically holding hands they were standing so close, and Harley looked as if she wanted to be sitting in Phoebe's lap.

"You're alive?" Phoebe asked.

"Somehow, yeah," Rose said.

"It's a Christmas miracle!" Phoebe said. "If you'd been gone thirty seconds longer, I'd have had all your worldly goods on eBay." Phoebe closed a tab on her PC.

"Look on the bright side," Bailey said. "We all make more money than Rose now. Tell us, what's it like not to have a job anymore?"

All eyes were on her, waiting for the story of how Vivian kicked her off the payroll. Rose shrugged. "Don't know. I've still got my job."

Everyone was silent until Phoebe spit out, "What?"

"She didn't fire me."

"Jesus!" Harley said. "How the hell did you get yourself out of this one, Walsh? What were you doing in there, blowing her?"

"No, she wanted me to use the dildo instead of my mouth."

Phoebe's jaw hung open.

"That was a joke."

A sigh of relief rocked the cubicle.

Harley still looked a little more impressed than before. "How'd you swing it then if you didn't get into her pants? There's no way it's not company policy to fire someone after they give you a dildo on the clock."

Everyone looked like they wanted an answer just as much as Harley did, and Rose didn't hesitate to tell them.

"She gave me drudge work as punishment. Also, I have a new office. Her storage closet."

Rose should have expected the outburst of laughter, especially from Phoebe.

"I never thought I'd see Rose Walsh back in the closet," Phoebe said. "When is she going to let you come out again?"

"Who knows? It's a good thing I'm quitting in a month, because I don't think I could stand to be cramped in there for much longer than that. And the worst part isn't even the storage closet. It's that I have to work right next to *Vivian*. She's about as much fun as you think she is."

"It doesn't look all bad. What's with the present?" Bailey asked, gesturing to the gift at her side. Rose had already forgotten about it.

"Oh, Vivian gave it to me," she said absentmindedly. Normally she was all about gifts, but normally she was also able to give people lists of what she wanted before they bought her anything. This was from a stranger who had no idea what she liked. It was probably a pair of socks with dancing snowmen on them.

"Vivian was your Secret Santa?" Mason asked.

"Oh, no. I just ran from the party before my Secret Santa could find me. They gave this to Vivian to pass on to me."

"Well, open it," Mason demanded. "It's Christmas, after all. And what better way to celebrate not getting fired than with presents?"

Rose humored him by tearing into the wrapping paper with less enthusiasm than she normally would. She wadded the snowflake-sprinkled paper into a ball and tossed it into the garbage bin before really looking at the gift in her hands.

"This...this is the exact same bath soap set I ordered for Vivian, only this person got theirs in the mail on time. Glad to know *that* idea was original. And now I have two of these. Looks like it's bubble baths only for me from now on. Good-bye, shower."

"Better than a dildo," Harley said.

This time Rose agreed. She kind of didn't want to see a sex toy ever again.

Or at least until she got another girlfriend.

"Well, anyway. I'm supposed to leave. Vivian wants me in her closet pronto. But I couldn't leave without telling you guys what happened first. I didn't want you all worrying about me all day."

"We appreciate it," Bailey told her.

"I'm going to miss you." Phoebe pouted. "What if my new cubemate sucks?"

"They probably will," Rose said. "It's hard to live up to my standards."

Phoebe pulled something off the wall, a piece of paper she wadded up and threw at Rose's nose.

Rose dodged the incoming projectile by catching it. When she unfolded it, she noted it was Garth's cell number. She did her best friend a favor and balled it up again before putting it in her pocket. She'd throw it away when she got home. Phoebe didn't need it anymore.

Chapter 3

VIVIAN'S IDEA OF A DESK was nothing more than a fold-up TV tray, and Rose plus the table took up all the space in the storage closet. An hour into her first full day of work by Vivian's side and her legs were already cramped. There wasn't even enough space to fit a desktop in the room. Vivian had handed her a small laptop to work on that looked suspiciously nice, meaning it was probably Vivian's personal property rather than anything given to her by the company. Rose was afraid she'd break it.

It was such a foreign feeling to have a working computer for once that she almost didn't know what to do with herself. It made work so much smoother, she could almost forget about the leg cramp. Too bad her job was boring as hell.

Rose found data entry less than thrilling, but at least she and Phoebe had a specific goal in mind when they set out on a day's work. Vivian had instructed Rose to sift through some financial reports, but she hadn't told Rose what she was supposed to be looking for. By noon, Rose was starting to think that she wasn't looking for anything. She was being sent on a wild goose chase, most likely Vivian's idea of a practical joke.

Until Rose found it.

Rose didn't even have to move an inch in order to poke her head out of the closet doorway. "Yo, I found something."

Vivian's face was buried in her ledgers. When she looked up, her brow was furrowed and her hair was almost as messy as Phoebe's on Monday morning after a weekend of drinking. She was haggard, and Rose wasn't about to improve her mood.

"Already?" she asked.

"If you think you can underestimate me, you've got a lot to learn. You've also got a problem."

Vivian rose from her desk, taking off her glasses and tossing them on top of her files. She was just barely able to squeeze into the closet with Rose. If Rose wasn't already claustrophobic, she was quickly developing symptoms.

"Look," Rose said, pointing at the screen.

"At what?" Vivian leaned down beside her until their heads were only inches apart. Whatever perfume she was wearing, it was much nicer than anything Rose owned. She let herself bask in the luxury of it for a moment.

"This is the number the board reported giving you at the start of the year. This is the number you actually got."

"That's…significantly less." That was putting it mildly. Vivian's eyes were frantically scouring the page, but Rose couldn't help but note how calm she was. "What else did you find?"

"There's only so much I can do with one branch's files. If our financial report was out of line with the company's, who knows if any of the other offices are getting their money either."

Vivian nodded silently, then walked back into her office. "Could you come here for a moment?"

Rose was happy to stretch her legs.

Vivian took a seat behind her desk while Rose stood to get her blood flowing again.

"I did what you told me to," Rose said. "So does this mean I get to keep my job?"

"Yes," Vivian stated clearly. "You still have a job here." She spoke slowly, choosing her words carefully and avoiding Rose's eye like she wasn't confident in what she was about to say. "Not only that, but I'm giving you a promotion."

"A promotion?"

"Yes. I would like for you to be my personal assistant."

That was far from a promotion in Rose's mind. "Your personal assistant?" Rose laughed. "You've got to be kidding. What do you want me to do, get you coffee? How do you take it? Black, two sugars, hold the dildo?"

Vivian didn't laugh. Rose tried to stop her own laughter.

"It's a temporary position," Vivian explained. "And a fake one. Next week I have a business meeting with Gene Giovani, the owner of the company, in New York. I need an excuse to bring you along with me so you can look through some of the company files."

"And we're getting these files how?" Rose asked.

"Because I know where they are."

"That sounds very vague and very illegal."

"And it's legal to embezzle funds?"

Vivian had a point. She also had a sound reason to investigate the company. Rose didn't. "Look, if you want to do that, I don't really care, but I don't want to be a part of it. I'm quitting to go back to school in a few weeks, and I don't want to get wrapped up in this. I looked at the numbers like you wanted me to, I apologized for the gag gift, and I just want to go back to data entry for the next few weeks so I can pay for my tuition."

Vivian sighed in frustration. "I don't like saying this, but I need someone like you with me who can look over the numbers as quickly as you just did. I can't do that on my own."

"Sucks for you," Rose said.

"I can give you a bonus."

"With what money? I saw your annual projections, remember."

"The money Gene gives us when I call him out for screwing us over."

"So the money you aren't guaranteed to get."

"Rose," Vivian pleaded. "You're my only option, and I don't know when I'm going to get another chance like this. Don't those numbers intrigue you? Do you not care what happens to everyone else working here? There's nothing I can do to get you to come along?"

Guilt trip. Ouch. Of course Rose didn't want to see her friends out of work because of corporate greed. Of course she was fascinated by the numbers. Of course being Vivian's only hope inflated her ego. But there was only one thing she could think of that would actually convince her to go. "Give my mom my job when I quit. She used to be a secretary, and she's been out of work ever since the company she worked for went out of business. She's qualified."

Vivian eyed Rose, a hint of surprise in her eyes. Her shoulders seemed to relax almost instantly. "Is that it? You'll go?"

Rose didn't have to think long. If this did end in Rose's mom taking over her job and finally being able to support herself, Rose couldn't turn it down. Plus, it wasn't like she wouldn't have fun hacking into Gio Corp.'s financial reports.

"I get a free trip to New York? All inclusive?"

Vivian nodded. Her face was a tense mask of annoyance.

"Can't pass that up." Rose ignored the glower. "Sounds a hell of a lot better than going home and telling my mom I got fired, so I guess I'm in."

"Good," Vivian said. "We'll be leaving soon. I'll call you with the flight details once I arrange them."

"I don't remember giving you my number," Rose said.

Vivian stared at her until Rose remembered the papers on the desk.

"My file. Right. Never mind."

Vivian nodded once, firmly, but kept up her quiet routine. A woman of few words was not the kind of person Rose usually liked to hang out with, especially when she didn't even take the time to laugh at her jokes. Things were already awkward between them. Rose had a feeling this trip to New York with Vivian was going to be about as relaxing as visiting Garth's gym with Phoebe. She didn't know how she was going to tolerate sitting next to her for hours on a plane flight and then having to spend who knows how long traveling with her in New York. She was already dreading this trip and she needed time to think, to sort it all out in her head.

⸺◦◦⟨⟩◦◦⸺

The first thing Rose saw when she walked in the front door was her mom on the couch, with a laundry basket resting in Rose's regular seat.

"You're home early."

"Not really," Rose said. "It's five."

"Already?" Beth asked.

"Time flies when you're having fun?"

"I wouldn't call watching soap operas and doing laundry fun."

Rose plopped down on the couch and caught a glance of some medical drama playing out on the screen. Not her cup of tea.

"How was work?" Beth asked.

Rose hadn't mentioned the Christmas party or her punishment, but now that she had some good news she had no qualms about sharing it with her mom, even if she had to leave out a few of the sketchier details. "I got a promotion. Where's the remote?"

"You got a promotion?"

Beth looked surprised. Rose was only slightly offended.

"Yep," she bragged, patting the cushions around her. "The president wants me to be her assistant. We're flying out to New York next week for a business meeting."

"Really?" Now Beth was more than surprised, she was impressed. She made no mention of the remote, though. Apparently, it wasn't nearly as important to her as it was to Rose. "You went from doing data entry with Phoebe to assisting the president of the entire company?"

"No, the President of the United States," Rose deadpanned.

Beth looked a little less impressed after that. She rolled her eyes and scooted over as Rose continued her search beneath her ass.

"Now I don't know if you're lying to me so you can skip work and go to New York next week or if I should actually congratulate you on your promotion."

"Like I have the money to take a trip to New York on my own," Rose said. "I did get the promotion. You don't have to believe me if you don't want to, but that doesn't change the fact that I am going to New York with my boss next week." Beth still looked suspicious. Rose would have let her think whatever she wanted if she wasn't afraid she'd never hear the end of it if her mom really thought she was skipping work. "Trust me, I wish I was going alone. It's not exactly going to be a vacation. My boss is a stuck-up bitch."

"How very nice of you to say."

"Just telling it like it is. It's not like she can hear me. I can't get fired or anything."

"You can if she overhears you talking like that at work."

"She won't. I'm on my best behavior for the last few weeks I'm there. Plus, if this trip goes well, there's another perk."

"What is it?" Beth asked.

Rose failed to hold back a smile. "My boss says she'll give you my job."

Beth's eyes went wide. "You got me a job?"

"Yep. As long as everything goes well. It's not the greatest place to work, and it doesn't pay a ton, but it's better than nothing. You'll get to work with Phoebe, too."

"Rose, I don't know what to say. Do I need to go in for an interview? Do I need to meet this woman?"

"Trust me, it's better if you don't meet Vivian. And no. I put in a good word for you, and that was enough. She owed me a favor."

"Do I want to ask what you did for her to deserve that favor?"

"Probably best if you didn't," Rose said.

Beth nodded. "I don't know how to thank you, Rose."

"No need to thank me, Mom. I'm just helping out." Rose gave up on finding the remote. "Apparently I'm not meant to watch TV, so I guess I'll go pack instead." When she stood from the couch, Rose immediately saw the remote. It had been in the one place she hadn't looked. Under her *own* ass. Oh well. The remote had won and she was too frustrated with it to want it now. She let it be and stretched out her legs again.

"When do you leave?" Beth asked.

"I don't know exactly. I'll tell you when my boss calls me with the details."

"Well, how long are you going to be gone?"

"I don't know exactly. I'll tell you when my boss calls me with the details."

"You sound very prepared."

"I'll figure it out."

"I sure hope so," Beth said. "Speaking of prepared, I hope you didn't need that second package you had coming in the mail. I put it in the bathroom. I forgot to tell you about it. It really was soap, thank God."

Of course. A day late. That was just Rose's luck.

Chapter 4

"I NEED YOU TO BE AT the airport by six."

"Please tell me you mean p.m."

"No."

Rose pinched the bridge of her nose. "You couldn't have picked a later flight?"

"I could have picked the four-thirty flight."

"Wow, I take it back. You're truly my hero. Because of you I'll get a whole half night's sleep. Now I only have to wake up at four instead of sitting up all night."

"If you're packed and ready to go it should be easy."

"Trust me, if you want me to be awake and functioning by 6:00 a.m., I'm going to need to chug at least three pots of coffee, which is going to take me some time to brew, not to mention all the time I'll have to spend in the bathroom after drinking three pots of coffee. Plus I need to get dressed and—"

"I don't need to hear your bleating. I just need you to be there. And I mean it, Rose. I *need* you there. You cannot be late."

"I won't, all right? Don't worry. I got this."

Rose glanced at her closet, currently scattered across her entire room. She was allowed one suitcase.

She still had twelve hours. She could do it.

If she didn't sleep at all.

"You've printed out your ticket, right?" Vivian asked.

"Yep."

"And you have it somewhere where you won't forget it?"

"Yep."

"And you have a ride to the airport tomorrow?"

"Yes, Mom, I do."

"I'm not your mother," Vivian snapped. "I'm your boss, and I'm responsible for your ability to show up at the airport on time and get on that plane with me so we can make this meeting go smoothly. If I was your mother, we wouldn't be in this situation. Unless you give your family members sex toys for Christmas as well."

"I got my mom a cute sweater, thank you very much. And are we really supposed to be talking about this on the company line?" Rose snapped. "What if Gene taps the phones and hears you talking about sex toys with your employees?"

"I'm not on the company line," Vivian said. "This is my personal number. And by the way, save it into your phone in case we get separated in New York. Or if you don't show up to the airport on time."

"I'll be there," Rose repeated for what felt like the hundredth time this week.

Vivian sighed. "I just want to make sure. You're the most crucial part of this plan, whether I want to admit that or not. If you're not there, it won't work."

"Then maybe you should trust me."

"I don't," Vivian said point blank. "You're my least-trusted employee. Need is not the same as trust."

"Whatever." Rose sighed, picking up another shirt from her bed and tossing it into the "no" pile.

"Would you like for me to call you in the morning and wake you up?"

Nothing sounded worse.

"No, Vivian. I can get myself up. There's this cool feature they have on phones now called an *alarm clock*. You should check it out sometime."

Rose swore she heard the wet slap of Vivian's eye roll.

"Good-bye, Rose." Vivian cut off the call so abruptly Rose could imagine her thumb pressing straight through the screen, shattering it cleanly like a bullet hole.

She hoped Vivian's phone was broken now. That way she would stop calling her every fucking minute about their stupid flight details. They'd been over them so many times they were tattooed onto Rose's mind.

Rose sorted through a few more shirts, convincing herself she was making more progress than she was before she dialed a number that was definitely not Vivian's. She made a mental note to save Vivian's number, if only because it would give her so much joy to block it later after she'd skipped out of Gio Corp.'s doors for the last time.

"Hey, Phoebe. What's up?"

"Well, it's six thirty on a Friday night, and you immediately assumed I didn't have plans and called me, so I'm kind of offended."

"Oh shit. Sorry," Rose said. "Am I interrupting something?"

"Not yet," Phoebe told her. "I have a date with Harley at seven, though."

"Congrats! So you guys are officially a thing now?"

It had only been a week since Rose had been bricked up alive in Vivian's closet, and she was missing so much. Catching up with Phoebe made her realize that being closer to her friend was why she had taken this job in the first place. Nothing said bonding quite like spending four hours a day trapped with your best friend in a five by five square. Now that Rose had lost that aspect of her job, she felt completely out of sync with Phoebe and the office gossip.

"We're going out to dinner," Phoebe told her. "Nothing too fancy. It's only the first date. Speaking of, how's your date with Vivian coming along?"

Phoebe couldn't see her, but Rose was scowling. "It's a business trip."

"Uh-huh," Phoebe taunted. "A business trip where you get all up in her business."

"Stop," Rose protested. "It's not like that."

"Sure. You give your boss a dildo and now all of sudden she's taking you on a 'business' trip to New York? Sounds like a sugar mama if you ask me."

"We're going for work," Rose said.

"Reeeally?" Phoebe drawled. "Because you still haven't told me what exactly your job is."

"It's confidential."

"You always were one to keep your sex life private."

"I'm hanging up," Rose said.

"That's fine. You called me," Phoebe reminded her. "Shouldn't you be packing for your date anyway?"

"Bye, Phoebe," Rose said sternly.

When she hung up, Rose shut off her phone for good. She had to finish packing before she let herself get distracted again.

⤙⬥⬥⬦⬥⬥⤚

"You're late."

"It's 6:02."

Vivian glanced at her watch. "6:02:08."

"You have a watch that counts seconds?"

"Yes, and you're currently wasting ones we don't have by asking me that question."

"Your answer took way longer than my question," Rose countered. "But whatever. Where's our gate?"

"It's on the west side of the building."

"Your watch got a compass too?"

"No. Now let's go."

For someone carrying a suitcase that was slightly larger than Rose's, Vivian sure moved quickly. Rose struggled to keep pace. She wheeled her luggage behind her between the crowds, navigating the airport as inexpertly as she navigated the office. Vivian's legs were just too long and those couple of inches she had over Rose were really making a difference.

42

"Slow down, Sonic. We're looking for the baggage check, not gold rings."

"I don't want to waste time," Vivian told her, slowing down a bit even though it looked as if it physically pained her to do so.

"Relax. We'll make it there on time. The plane doesn't take off till seven. What are the chances our flight gets delayed and we'll have all kinds of extra time anyway?"

"Don't say that," Vivian scolded. "We're supposed to check into our hotel by afternoon."

"You realize the flight time from DC to New York is like an hour, right? They can delay us till ten and we would still make it to the hotel on time."

"Anything can go wrong between now and then, Rose," Vivian said. "We have no idea how long it'll take to get out of the airport once we get to New York, and then we actually have to find the hotel." Vivian sighed. "I just want things to go as smoothly as possible."

"And they will. If you relax. You're stressing yourself out over nothing."

"Well, one of us has to stay on top of things. It's certainly not going to be you. You couldn't even answer your phone this morning when I called you."

"I was busy talking to the cab driver. I didn't hear it ring." Actually, she had accidentally put her phone in silent mode while trying to turn off her alarm that morning, but she wasn't eager to admit that mistake.

The line for the X-ray scanner was moving faster than the one for baggage scanning. Barely. As their suitcases passed through the scanner, Vivian began to look even more anxious than usual. Rose couldn't tell if she was just giddy to finally be getting out of here or if she was genuinely nervous about airport security screening. Either way, if she didn't start meeting the TSA agents' eyes and playing it cool, they were both going to be "randomly selected" for full-on pat downs.

Fortunately, no one else thought Vivian was acting as weird as Rose did.

Those were the benefits of being white. And well-dressed.

"Hurry up," Vivian called, her bags already in hand as Rose struggled to put her shoes back on.

"It's six thirty in the morning," Rose groaned. "Most of the world isn't even awake yet. Be glad I'm moving at all."

Vivian pouted while Rose grabbed her bag. She looked slightly happier when they started to move again, and Rose realized that Vivian never looked particularly comfortable no matter what situation they were in.

"Some of us aren't wearing slip-ons," she said.

"Yes, you're more familiar with strap-ons," Vivian muttered under her breath.

More dildo jokes. And this time completely offhand. Rose would almost consider humoring her with a response if Vivian hadn't meant it as an insult. She had, though. She could tell just by her tone. This wasn't some harmless quip from Phoebe, and Rose wouldn't banter with her like they were friends. She couldn't and wouldn't let Vivian rile her up when she wanted to. Rose wouldn't give her the satisfaction, so she pretended not to hear.

Rose felt like they'd been sitting at the gate for ages. Vivian was surprisingly calm, and if this was how long all flights took, then Rose was happy she didn't have the money to travel. When they called first class, Rose jumped up from her seat.

Vivian shot an arm out to stop her. "What are you doing?"

Rose looked at her like she was mad. "They're boarding first class," she explained. "Come on."

Vivian didn't remove her arm.

Rose tried everything to stop the very bad feeling forming in the pit of her stomach. It didn't work.

"Vivian," she drawled, speaking as slowly as possible to make sure their conversation was clear. "Why aren't you letting me go?"

Vivian shook her head. Her dark curls bounced lightly against the shoulder of her button-up as she fed Rose the scariest three-word sentence she'd ever heard. "We're in coach."

"Please, tell me you didn't just say that."

"We couldn't afford to bring luggage," Vivian pointed out. "You know more than anyone what's happened to our budget, and you think we were able to afford first class tickets?"

Rose hadn't actually looked at her ticket stub. She had merely assumed they were flying first class. Vivian was a civilized person. The CEO of the company was paying for them. Rose thought for sure that she'd finally get her chance to fly in the lap of luxury.

"I am so fixing this." Rose said it like a promise. She hoped Vivian took it like one.

The gate agent announced it was coach's turn to board.

Vivian followed her out for a change, struggling to keep up with Rose's power walk.

When Rose dreamed of flying, she always had the window seat. She wanted to look outside, see the world from a point of view she could only otherwise experience in pictures. Everything looked different from an aerial perspective—smaller, shorter, like heads floating without bodies. Houses were roofs. Skyscrapers were single floors. She figured she'd spend her flights sketching or taking pictures from above the plane's wings. But on this, her first flight, she took the aisle seat and forced Vivian to experience the wonder of the skies from the window seat. Rose had more important matters to attend to.

They were two of the first people to find their seats in coach, and the aisles beside them were crowded long after they placed their carry-ons in the cubby holes above them and sat down. When the mob settled, Rose flagged down a flight attendant with conviction.

The woman who came to assist her was a young blonde who rocked the airline outfit like it was a knock-off, overly sexualized

Halloween costume. It clung to her succulent ass as if she worked as a bachelorette party stripper. She was very, very cute, to say the least. Rose could work with it.

"Excuse me…Heather." Rose read the stewardess's name tag. She popped her best flirty smile. "There was a bit of a mix-up with our tickets. See, we were supposed to be flying first class, but our intern accidentally purchased coach. And I know it's a short flight, and I know you have dozens of other people trying to weasel their way into first class without a ticket, but we fly a lot for our job. We're actually on a business trip right now to New York. Ms. Tracey is the president of a major corporation in DC, and I'm her personal assistant," Rose explained, pointing to Vivian, then herself. "We're very busy people, but I'm sure that if we encountered an airline along the way to our meeting that was able to accommodate us and help us correct this little problem we're having, that we would almost certainly find the time to recommend it to all of our colleagues, as well as call the airline and let them know what wonderful flight attendants they have. So what do you think? Can you can help us out, Heather?"

Rose ended her request with the biggest, most manipulative smile she could project. Heather looked between the two women in the seats, summing them up like a math problem. Vivian wasn't smiling like Rose was. In fact, she scowled like a woman who had been put in coach class and wasn't amused about it. She looked aloof, angry, and professional, and that was all Rose needed her to do in order to back up the charade. Enough of the lie had been truth that as long as they played their parts well, Heather had no reason not to believe them.

She set her hand over Rose's on the seat rest and smiled back at her. "I'll see what I can do."

With one not-so-subtle squeeze to Rose's hand, she was gone.

"I can't believe you lied to that girl," Vivian scolded as soon as she was gone, ducking her head and whispering so as not to alert Heather or any nearby passengers who might rat out their scheme.

"We *are* on a business trip. You *can* tell everyone in the office that the airline is good. Geez. Don't get your panties in a bunch."

Vivian was far too serious about this. "Just be glad I assisted you into possibly getting first-class seats." Heather floated back with an extra pep in her step.

"You're in luck!" she sang happily. "There are a couple of free seats in first class. You're welcome to take them if you'd like."

"We would love to!" Rose cut Vivian off before she could decline the offer just to spite Rose or clear her conscience or whatever stupid reason she probably had floating around in her head. "Let's get our bags, Viv."

Rose was out of her seat before Vivian had time to cringe at the nickname.

"You're a doll, Heather," Rose said, placing her hand delicately on the woman's arm. "Will you be serving us in first class as well?"

"Of course, miss." Heather nodded sheepishly, the natural red of her cheeks suddenly overpowering the red of the blush caked on them. "I'm sorry, I didn't catch your name."

"I'm Rose, and this is Vivian," she said. "Thanks again, Heather."

"It's no problem, Rose. Let me show you your seats."

First class was everything Rose had dreamed of and more. The chairs were cushioned and ergonomic, the gap between aisles was the size of the Grand Canyon, and the first thing Heather did when she escorted them to their seats was slap a breakfast menu down on their trays.

"I'll be back in just a bit," Heather told them. "Let me know what you want to eat."

"Oh, I sure will." Rose winked.

Heather walked away, blushing more furiously than ever.

"You didn't need to flirt with her again," Vivian said, even crankier than normal. "She'd already gotten us into first class."

"So what?" Rose shrugged. "Nothing wrong with a little flirting. I'd even find *you* cute if you got me free breakfast and a comfortable chair."

Now it was Vivian's turn to blush. Or maybe she was just red from fuming. Either way, she went quiet, and Rose was happy to sink into her chair and enjoy the moment of relaxation.

Chapter 5

THE CAB DRIVER LEFT THEM stranded in the parking lot, standing by a mountain of shoveled snow. Without stopping to distribute their luggage, Vivian carried both bags into the lobby of the hotel by herself. Rose followed closely behind her, not minding that Vivian had offered to carry everything, but when Vivian finally handed Rose her suitcase, she handed her own luggage over along with it.

"Take these. We're in 210."

Rose took the suitcases with a grunt. They weren't that heavy. She could easily wheel both of them around. She just didn't want to. "Why do I have to carry them? Why can't you do it?"

"Because I have to check in and see if there are any messages from Gene," Vivian pulled her wallet out of her pocket and her ID out of the leather pouch. "Unless you'd like to flirt with the clerk and see if you can upgrade our room to a suite."

Rose rolled her eyes and extended the handles on the bags. "No, thanks."

"What's wrong?" Vivian asked, eying the young boy in a suit and tie behind the counter. "Not into men?"

"I'm your assistant, not a prostitute."

"Fine, then please *assist* me by taking our bags to our room while I take care of this. Online it says our room is 210. I have to get the key cards."

"Fine."

The elevator ride was musty and claustrophobic, and Rose was happy to be deposited onto the second floor. After a couple of inhales, though, she realized the air in the hotel wasn't as fresh as she had originally thought, and she blamed Vivian for being stingy in picking such a cheap place. The hall smelled of stale cigarettes and bar crawlers making their way back to their rooms early in the morning after a long night. Still, it was better than the elevator. A sense of liberty washed over her. Maybe she didn't come to New York entirely for fun, but that didn't mean she couldn't have a little of it. Maybe she could even do it with someone by her side. The bar scene here had to be better than back in DC.

Room 210 wasn't far from the elevator, a fact that was both a blessing and a curse in Rose's mind. Lord knew she didn't want to travel far to get to the elevator every time she needed to go downstairs to leave, but if anyone else staying on this floor was anything like Rose, she and Vivian would be hearing a lot of noise disturbance outside their room in the middle of the night as the clubbers returned from the streets. Rose could live with it. If she had anything to say about it, she'd be stumbling back to the hotel late herself.

Vivian, on the other hand... Vivian would just have to deal with it.

Then she realized she had no key. Rose slouched down in front of the door like a dog waiting to be let inside. She rested her head back and debated taking a quick nap while she waited for Vivian to show up with the key, but again, Vivian was speedier than Rose anticipated. A shadow ascending the staircase on the opposite end of the hallway caught Rose's eye, and Vivian emerged around the corner moments later. She gripped the key card in her hand like it was more important not to lose than her credit card.

"You took the stairs?" Rose questioned, too tired to disguise the disapproval in her tone.

"We only had to go up one floor," Vivian said. "And yes, I try to take the stairs whenever I can. It's healthier. It also didn't help that the elevator looked a bit rickety."

Rose was pretty sure no one had said the word "rickety" since the 1950s.

"It smelled like ass," Rose said, using the correct terminology for this century. "I almost wanted it to break down and kill me."

Vivian looked more than uncomfortable. Her face did that pouty thing, and she didn't seem like she wanted to tolerate their conversation any longer.

"Move so I can open the door."

Rose scooted over, back shifting against the wall instead of the doorframe, but that didn't stop Vivian's ass from being two inches in front of her face while she unlocked the door. Rose didn't mind as much as she thought she would.

Vivian worked the key card like a pro, letting herself in on the first try. It always took Rose at least six.

The room was…all right. It wasn't the luxury Rose was hoping for, but it was slightly bigger than her bedroom at home, and even if she did have to share it with Vivian, it at least had a kitchen and bathroom attached to it, something she didn't even have available at her mother's house.

Vivian took the bed closest to the door. Rose took the bed closest to the window. The room was so small, though, that the beds were practically bumping against one another. Only a small night stand separated them, and if they didn't sleep on complete opposite sides of their beds, it would almost feel like they were sharing one. Rose wasn't looking forward to rolling over in the middle of the night and watching Vivian snore three feet away from her.

Vivian's ass was a better view than the window offered. Rose was expecting a stunning glimpse of the skyline, but they weren't high up enough to see New York in all its glory. Vivian's voice tore her away from the window.

"We have a meeting at headquarters at one."

"Okay," Rose said, running a hand through her locks to straighten them back to their normal curl. No doubt her hair and her eyes still looked puffy from lack of sleep, but by the time they got to headquarters she should have had enough time to rejoin the living instead of looking like one of the living dead. "I'm ready to go."

Vivian looked her up and down.

"Like what you see?" Rose asked, raising an eyebrow to go along with it.

"No." Vivian spoke honestly. "You can't wear that."

Rose looked down. She was still in the clothes she had worn to the airport, the same clothes that had convinced the flight attendant on the plane that she was in the entourage of the president of a major company in DC. "What's wrong with them?"

"They're disheveled. It's not professional. Please go straighten yourself up in the bathroom."

Rose took the order, but she also took offense. She'd gay herself up in the bathroom instead.

Looking in the mirror, maybe her clothes were a bit more unkempt than she'd thought they were, which mostly meant that her neckline was halfway around her shoulder and somehow the top button of her blouse had come undone. She straightened the fabric out and ran a hand along the front of her shirt, smoothing out as many wrinkles as she could. It wasn't perfect, but it was better, and with a quick brush to her hair and a small coat of mascara to her lashes, she even looked cleaned up enough for Vivian.

They were in a cab in no time and at headquarters even sooner than that. The New York office was so much bigger than the DC one that Rose was stunned. If the embezzled money was going back to the company instead of a person, Rose wouldn't be surprised if the entire sum went to this place's rent.

Vivian led her down hallways and past office rooms like a pro, up to the third floor and into a conference room where two men were waiting for them. They both stood from their chairs at Vivian's entrance, and the older one was the first to approach them with a smile.

"Vivian. It's great to see you again." Gene spoke kindly, wrapping both of his hands around Vivian's outstretched one as he greeted her. Rose liked him immediately. The smile lines on his face were genuine, not the result of decades of scowling, which was exactly what the younger man beside him was doing when he stepped closer.

"It's great to see you again too, Mr. Giovanni," Vivian said.

"Please." He smiled wider. "You know by now to call me Gene."

"This is my new assistant, Rose Walsh. Rose, this is Gene and Nick Giovanni."

There was no doubt Nick was Gene's son. They had the same slicked-back hair, the same expensive suit, the same wide-set jaw, and the same sharp-tipped nose. The only thing they didn't share was the jagged scar above Nick's lip. Rose wondered what the story was there.

"It's nice to meet you," Rose said. Gene shook Rose's hand the same way he shook Vivian's, the smile never leaving his face. Rose couldn't imagine him embezzling funds from his own company. He was already off her suspects list.

Nick's mood seemed to improve the moment he saw Rose. Unabashedly, he looked her up and down, eyes lingering far too long at her neckline. His scar curved into a hook when he smiled.

"It's *very* nice to meet you," he said, and if his sudden shift in tone wasn't enough to creep Rose out, watching his lip scar caress her skin as he lifted her hand to his mouth for a kiss certainly did the trick.

Rose looked to Vivian for help only to find Vivian looking back at her with concern in her eyes.

"Rose has some work to do for me during the meeting," Vivian said, distracting Nick and causing him to drop Rose's hand. "I'm just going to show her my office and will be back quickly."

Vivian wrapped an arm around Rose's waist, ready to usher her out of the room.

"I can show the pretty lady around," Nick offered.

Rose grimaced. "No thank you," she said. "The pretty lady would rather have the other pretty lady show her around." Rose tugged on Vivian's hand, and the look of contempt on Nick's face as he looked toward Vivian didn't go unnoticed by Rose.

"I'll be right back," Vivian said again, this time to Gene, not Nick.

Vivian linked her arm in Rose's and all but dragged her down the hall. As soon as they were out of earshot of the Giovannis, Rose said, "Nick's a dick."

"Trust me, I know." The exasperated sigh that followed told Rose this was not the first time Vivian had put up with him. "Unfortunately, he's head of the Boston branch, so he's around more than I'd like him to be. He's almost as unprofessional as you, and if he wasn't Gene's son, there's no way he'd be as high on the ladder as he is."

Vivian's slander of her professionalism didn't escape Rose. She was going to argue that at least she didn't sexually harass women she'd never met before, but then she remembered how she'd ended up as Vivian's sidekick in the first place. If she couldn't condemn Nick's behavior, she could at least criticize the next most important thing. His looks.

"Not to be rude or anything," Rose started, channeling every straight person who had ever confronted her about her sexuality. "But what's with his lip? It looks like he hit on the wrong girl and she decked him in the face. I'm about to do the same to the other side of his mouth."

"It's worse than that," Vivian said. "When he got the cut last spring, he said it came from one of his dogs. I wouldn't be surprised if he fights them."

"Yikes. He's even uglier on the inside than he is on the out. And that's saying something."

Vivian led Rose to a room at the end of the hall. It was undeniably Vivian's office. Boring. Clinical. A "V. Tracey" name plaque on the door. The decked out, technical home base of espionage movies it was not. Rose's inner spy was disappointed.

"Take my laptop and my pass key," Vivian said. "I barely use this office, but maybe you can find something in the files or an email. All my passwords are in a document on my laptop. You should have no problems getting into everything."

First snooping on company files and now getting access to Vivian's personal computer? Maybe Rose could have some fun with this after all.

"You don't have forever, though," Vivian warned. "Copy what you'll need and don't waste time. I don't expect lunch to last long."

"I got it," she promised. "I'll be done in a jiffy."

A jiffy? Now she was speaking in retro terms. Vivian was already rubbing off on her, and not in a good way.

Vivian left Rose to her own devices, and she set up shop at Vivian's desktop, quickly scouring Vivian's laptop for her login info. She found it in a document labeled "Passwords." *Genius.* Hopefully, Vivian had more virus protection than she had subtlety.

The first thing Rose noticed about Vivian's desktop was the layer of dust coating the monitor. The second thing she noticed was that it didn't suck. It was a newer model than anything she'd seen at the DC office, and that told Rose one thing. The NY office did not have the money problems theirs did. It did have information, though. Vivian's hard drive was full of old financial reports for all of Gio's branches. It went back years. No doubt most of the information was extraneous, but at least she could pinpoint exactly when DC's budget started falling and if any other offices were crashing along with it. Maybe Vivian could correlate the dates to an event or a new hire among the higher-ups. She set about transferring all the reports she could find onto her flash drive.

Rose was so in the zone that a sudden *ping* made her jump. Paranoid, she searched the screen frantically for a security popup to notify her of her blocked access, but she quickly realized the noise had come from Vivian's laptop, not her desktop. Rose didn't mean to snoop, but she couldn't help but eye the screen and the email popup in the corner of it. Jana's name was listed as the sender.

"How's the meeting, babe?"

Babe? Rose hovered over the contact name. The email address was connected to Gio's website. This was definitely the Jana Rose had met at the office, but this was definitely not a professional email.

Another *ping* shook Rose, this time to alert her that her files were finished downloading.

Rose didn't have time to investigate anything any further. Through the window of the office she could see Vivian approaching, Gene and Nick on her tail.

Rose shut the laptop inconspicuously, removed her flash drive from the desktop, and slid it into her pocket. She slipped out of the office just as calmly and met the group before they could catch her in the act.

"Get everything done?" Vivian asked.

"Yep," Rose said.

"Good." Vivian gave her a nod of approval. "We should get going."

"It was nice meeting you, Rose." Gene gave Rose a smile then turned toward Vivian. "I look forward to our meeting on Monday."

"That makes one of us," Nick added. His face was so stony. Rose couldn't tell if it was supposed to be a joke or not.

Vivian didn't seem to think so. Her smile was so forced Rose thought she was going to break character. Rose nearly applauded her when she didn't. "It was a pleasure as always, Mr. Giovanni."

"Are you sure you found everything you needed?"

"Everything and more," Rose promised, thinking of that email from Jana.

The cab ride back to the hotel hadn't been fun. Vivian was crankier than usual, and when they made it back to their room she practically stabbed the key card into its slot.

Rose figured now was an appropriate time to further ruin Vivian's mood by complaining.

"This room is really small," Rose said. "I can't believe we have to share this for an entire week. We don't even get our own bathrooms." She collapsed onto her bed and used Vivian's mattress as a footstool. Rose's tired feet were probably not the most disgusting thing that mattress had seen lately.

"It's the best I could do with our budget," Vivian said. "Don't blame me. Blame Nick."

"Nick?" Rose asked. She sat up, intrigued.

"I'm pretty sure he's our embezzler."

Somehow Rose wasn't surprised.

"I need a drink," Rose said, walking over to the mini bar. For such a cheap room, the price for a packet of Reese's Cups or a single beer seemed outrageous. She gripped the neck of a vodka bottle tentatively.

"You paying for that?" Vivian asked.

"No," Rose admitted, taking her hand off the bottle and closing the fridge. "Let's go out. It'll be cheaper. And we can relax."

Vivian stared at her for so long that Rose started to wonder if she even knew what relaxation was. "Maybe later," Vivian said. "When it's not two p.m."

Rose couldn't really argue with that.

Chapter 6

"I have nothing to wear," Rose complained. Her suitcase was small, and she had packed for business, not pleasure. Her outfits were made to keep her warm and professional, not to dress her up for a night on the town.

"I brought extra clothes," Vivian said. "You can borrow something if you need to."

Vivian was already rifling through her suitcase, and Rose wanted to stop her before she wasted her time, knowing that was one of Vivian's biggest pet peeves. "Thanks, but, no offense, I don't think your shirts would fit me. My boobs are a little bigger than yours." A little bigger was an understatement, but Rose didn't have to brag about it. She didn't need to make the girl feel bad about herself.

"I know."

Rose raised an eyebrow at that. "You know? Have you been looking?"

Rose's comment was a joke, mostly, but Vivian was still embarrassed. She covered her tracks quickly. "I made you fix your outfit before we left. It was kind of hard not to notice."

Fair point. Rose dropped it.

Vivian didn't stop rummaging through her suitcase, though. Rose was starting to wonder if it was an unconscious action at this point, an excuse to keep her occupied and not looking Rose in the eye. A few seconds later, however, Vivian handed her a dark, lacy blouse and a black bra to match. The bra was definitely closer to Rose's size than Vivian's own.

Rose took the outfit tentatively and held the bra in front of her face. "Why did you buy this if it isn't your size?"

"It's not mine."

Vivian offered nothing else, and that single sentence did little to clear Rose's confusion. "You packed another woman's clothes?"

"It's Jana's," Vivian said, as if that cleared up everything.

"Ok, but why do you have her bra?"

"I packed weeks ago when I thought she was coming instead of you. I forgot to take her stuff out of my suitcase."

Of course Vivian had packed literally *weeks* in advance. But why had she packed *Jana's* stuff in the first place?

Rose tried exhaustively to make sense of this.

"So you're telling me that weeks ago Jana made a point of giving you whatever she was going to take on the trip so that you could put it in your suitcase?" Surely the company wasn't that stingy. They could have each brought their own separate luggage like Vivian and Rose had. "And then after she decided not to go," she continued, "she completely spaced that she left her stuff with you and didn't ask for it back? You don't think she noticed that her toothbrush was missing or does she just not brush her teeth?"

"I'm sure she has an extra toothbrush," Vivian deadpanned. "And, yes, that's exactly what happened."

Rose didn't buy that for a second. Not after that email she'd found on Vivian's computer.

Vivian was too quick to change the subject. She ran a hand through the thickness of her hair, an action that started out as a calming motion, but ended with retracting her fingers with a frown. "I need to shower. I'll try not to use all of those little bottles of shampoo, but I kind of have a lot of hair so no promises."

"Don't bother." Rose raced to her own suitcase, digging around in the front pouch until she found her toiletry bag and the bath kit inside it that she had bought for Vivian. She handed her the bundle of products. They weren't wrapped like she wanted them to be, but it would have to do. "This was your real Christmas present. Sorry I didn't have it ready in time."

Vivian turned the package over in her hands, observing it like conditioner was a novel concept. She looked back up to Rose with a quirk in her brow. "Did you re-gift this?"

Jesus. Rose knew her own Secret Santa had had the same idea as her and given her the exact set of soaps, but how many other women had Vivian seen opening this very bath kit in the break room at the Christmas party? Did Bath and Body Works only make this one product now? Did women ever get any gifts other than soap?

"No," Rose said honestly. "But apparently it was a popular gift choice. My Secret Santa got me the same thing. I guess I know better than to buy the very first thing Bath and Body Works advertises on their website from now on. The dildo was a bit more creative."

"Well, the shampoo is a bit more useful," Vivian countered. "So thank you."

"No problem."

Watching Vivian gather a change of clothes and a clean towel made Rose realize how much she needed a shower, too. She'd bathed this morning before she left for the airport, but traveling for so long and being around Nick made her feel gross.

Vivian noticed her fidgeting and apparently was capable of being sympathetic.

"Do you want to get in the shower first?"

Rose was very eager to jump on that opportunity, but before she could open her mouth to tell Vivian thanks, her phone buzzed in her pocket. She pulled it out to look at it before giving Vivian an answer. There was one new text message in her notifications.

"U ded?"

Rose had completely forgotten to call Phoebe and tell her she landed safely. Between traveling and snooping around headquarters, she just hadn't had the time. She'd do it now.

"No, you go ahead and shower first," Rose told Vivian. "I'll get in after you and then we can go somewhere. Celebrate."

Vivian nodded in agreement. They still had a lot to accomplish on this trip, but Rose finally had access to the files they needed. Even someone like Vivian knew that even the smallest victories deserved celebration.

Rose just hoped Vivian could handle her idea of a good time.

***

"Hey, Pho."

"Oh, wow, you finally called. It's only like two thirty. What time did we agree on again? Ten o'clock? I didn't know I meant p.m. when I said that."

Phoebe didn't sound honestly annoyed, but Rose apologized anyway. "I know. I'm sorry, Pho. I just got sidetracked. Vivian and I had to go to this business meeting, and we just got back. I met the owner, and he's a great guy, but his son is a total jerk off."

"High school Rose was quite fond of jerking off, if I remember correctly," Phoebe chastised.

"If only college Phoebe was fond of *fucking* off," Rose countered.

"Oh don't worry. College Phoebe did plenty of fucking last night," she bragged. "I'm still at Harley's apartment. She's in the shower."

Rose glanced to her own hotel bathroom, where, judging by the sound of running water, Vivian was still in the shower, too.

Good. She didn't need Vivian overhearing that two of her employees were hooking up. Coworker relationships were strictly against company policy—not that Vivian followed that particular rule herself, apparently. Because of her relationship with Jana, Vivian had no leverage to report anything even if she did find out about Harley and Phoebe. But Rose would rather be safe than sorry.

She walked as far away from the bathroom door as she could, settling on the mattress of her own bed and pulling back the curtains so she could watch the sunlight leak in and wash over the leg of her pants.

"Congrats, Pho!" she exclaimed. "How is she in bed?"

Phoebe's voice was low, sultry, like she and Harley had just finished an encore of what had no doubt happened the night before. "Let's just say her hands are good for more than fixing electronics."

"Have I told you how jealous I am?" Rose thumped the back of her skull against the headboard as she reclined, as if the pain would distract her from her sexual frustration. "At this point, I can't even remember the last time I got laid."

"You should find someone," Phoebe said. "New York is your oyster, you know?"

She and Phoebe were on the same wavelength, but, then again, when weren't they?

"Trust me, I am very aware, and I vow to take advantage of that. I just have to be a little more careful than usual. I share a room with Vivian, so I don't think she'd appreciate the free show if I brought someone home and banged them all night while she was trying to sleep ten feet away from us. And I'm not going to go home with someone who knows I'm a tourist and will have weeks to flee the country before the police finally ID my body buried in a dumpster in an alley somewhere."

"You're smart. You'll figure something out."

"Yeah."

Rose had been so caught up in her conversation with Phoebe that she hadn't heard the shower shut off. When she listened closely now, the room was silent apart from the hum of the heater and the occasional honk from the parking lot below. Vivian was going to burst through the bathroom door any minute.

"I've got to go," Rose said. "I'll text you later. Tell you how my night on the town goes."

"Try not to drunk text me," Phoebe warned. "It used to be cute, but it just gets sad after a while."

"I don't plan on getting too drunk. Can't really consent to sex or run away from a serial killer if I'm wasted, can I?"

"See? I told you you were smart."

"Thanks, Pho. Bye."

"Bye."

Rose hung up and plugged her phone into the nearest outlet. If she was going to be out all night, she needed a way to call 911 or fake drunk text Phoebe while she was still sober just for kicks if things weren't going well at the bar. She left it on her bedside table for safekeeping before gathering her clothes. She wanted that bathroom as soon as Vivian surrendered it.

Vivian wasn't quick to exit the bathroom, but when she did, she smelled sweet, like a fresh ocean breeze or dew drops dripping from a tropical palm leaf in the middle of a rainforest. That bath kit, however unoriginal a gift it may have been, had been a good call.

Rose couldn't tell if she really liked the way Vivian smelled or if she just couldn't wait to smell that way herself.

Something quickly distracted Rose from the sudden freshness of the room, though. As she watched Vivian pat the frizz of her hair dry with a crisp white towel, she noticed the second towel wrapped around her torso. She hadn't looked intentionally, but the two of them were crammed into the hallway between rooms together. They had practically bumped into each other on Vivian's way out of the restroom. It was kind of hard not to notice in such close proximity. It was the first time Rose had seen her in anything other than business attire, and, she had to say, the nude look suited Vivian. Her skin was still damp and pink from the steam, and it only seemed to redden more the longer Rose looked at her.

"Took you long enough," Rose scolded playfully, bringing her eyes back up to meet Vivian's.

Vivian's cheeks were as blushed as Rose expected them to be. She gripped her towel closer to her chest. "Sorry. It's all this hair. Takes a while to wash."

Vivian's hair was definitely long. Not "I grew up in a religious cult" long, but it was longer than Rose's blonde locks which were creeping down past her shoulders at this point. Rose might grow her own as long as Vivian's someday. It looked good on her.

"You're fine," she said, hoping not too much time had passed while she was unintentionally staring at Vivian. "Where do you want to go once we get ready?"

"Wherever you want."

"I've never been here before. You tell me where we should go out."

Vivian gnawed on her bottom lip. "Do you want to see the Statue of Liberty?"

Of course.

"When I said we could go out, I kind of meant 'go out.' Like, see the night life."

"It's three in the afternoon."

"Yeah, but by the time we both get ready it'll be later."

"How long do you take in the shower?" Vivian's tone was skeptical.

"Certainly not as long as you."

"Then it won't be that late. We could see the Statue of Liberty. Or the Empire State Building. Or something."

Rose cringed. "What are we, twelve? Can't we just go out like adults?"

Vivian gnawed on her bottom lip again, this time more anxiously. "I'm here on business, Rose. I don't feel comfortable inebriating myself while practically on the clock."

"But you're not on the clock," Rose reminded her. "And if you really thought you were here strictly on business, you wouldn't feel comfortable sightseeing either. What's the difference between having a couple beers at the bar or having a cup of hot chocolate in Central Park?"

"One you have to be twenty-one to do," Vivian quipped.

"And what do you know?" Rose said. "You're over twenty-one."

Vivian sighed, and Rose could tell that, once again, sassing her way through an argument wasn't the most reliable way to persuade her boss.

"Come on, Vivian. Tonight's the night to go out if we're going to do it. It's Saturday. We don't have a meeting till Monday. You can have a hangover all day tomorrow and no one will know. There won't be any consequences. We're leaving on Friday, and I'll never get a chance to experience New York's weekend nightlife if we don't do it now. Don't we deserve to celebrate Nick's inevitable downfall?"

Rose crossed her arms, waiting for an answer and hoping Vivian took her accusation as a challenge. Something told Rose Vivian couldn't back down when her own hypocrisy was thrust in front of her.

"Fine," Vivian agreed, though she wasn't quite happy about it. "But on one condition. If I go out with you and drink tonight, you have to come with me to Central Park beforehand. And buy me that hot chocolate. I demand you see more of New York than the inside of a bar."

Vivian drove a hard bargain. Rose might not be able to sympathize, but she could compromise. A couple mugs of hot chocolate wouldn't kill her. The snow might, though.

"Deal," she agreed, and she held out her hand for Vivian to shake. Business types like Vivian always took handshakes seriously. This way Rose knew Vivian wouldn't ditch her to run back to their hotel as soon as soon as they finished their cocoa.

Vivian's skin was still warm from the shower, and their touch purposefully lingered. With how sharp-edged Vivian's personality was, Rose didn't expect her to feel so soft and human. This was a much nicer side of her. One Rose could get used to.

Rose crashed that train of thought like a car with no brakes and focused on what else Vivian's warmth reminded her of.

"It's going to be colder than our fucking office outside," Rose warned. "You sure you don't want to go somewhere that has heating?"

Vivian shook her head. She had stopped trying to wrestle her hand away from Rose as soon as Rose had tightened her grip, but now Rose let go of Vivian of her own accord.

"I want you to see Central Park. It's beautiful in winter." Vivian was adamant.

"All right." Rose surrendered. If Vivian wanted her to be a tourist, then she'd damned well be a tourist. She made her way to the bathroom. "Let me get ready."

Chapter 7

"I can't feel my teeth."

Rose was bundled from head to toe, clothed in snow boots and gloves and a scarf atop the thickest coat she owned.

The walk in the park had been a walk in the park. Until it started to snow.

"Can you normally feel your teeth?" Vivian asked, subtly running her tongue along the inside of her mouth.

"I don't know, but I can hear them chattering. Aren't you supposed to be able to feel things that you can hear?"

"Ghosts?" Vivian proposed, more of a suggestion than a question.

"What? Do you even believe in ghosts?"

Vivian shrugged. "I don't know. It's the same as believing in luck or fate, right?"

Rose believed in fate. Ghosts, not so much.

"The difference between those two things is that you don't hear luck. People hear ghosts. Or claim to anyway. And for the record, people feel ghosts, too. They always talk about how the room gets all cold and shit when they sense a spirit nearby."

"I think Central Park might be a graveyard, then."

Rose was too cold to laugh at the joke for long. Her muscles were stiff. It sure did feel nice to have her body shudder because of something that wasn't the temperature, though.

"Drink some more cocoa," Vivian instructed. "That'll warm up your teeth."

The cup was too warm. If she drank all of her hot chocolate, the cup would go cool and what would warm her hands, then? Her gloves?

Rose didn't want to take the risk.

She took a small sip, though, and relished in the way it left a trail of heat blazing from the back of her tongue all the way down to her stomach.

Vivian had wanted to order hot chocolate from a local coffee shop, but Starbucks was closer and Rose wasn't walking that far out of her way. Plus she trusted it more. She could never go wrong with Starbucks, even if she could barely afford it.

"I hate you for this, you know?" Rose told her. "If you didn't make me go to Central Park I'd be warm right now."

"Be lucky you're here at all. I could've had you fired, remember? If you weren't here, you'd just be freezing your ass off in DC."

"I would be inside," Rose stressed. "No one is dumb enough to venture outside when it's fucking blizzarding. Look around!"

The command was mostly rhetorical. There was nothing to look at, but that was kind of Rose's point. There were people here of course—it was Central Fucking Park, of course there were other tourists desperate to cram in every site on their vacation, while everyone sane was at home or in their hotels.

Vivian didn't seem too pleased to have her intelligence questioned. She glared at Rose over her cup, but the chocolate mustache she was left with when she pulled it away from her face was not very intimidating.

Rose laughed again. Vivian wiped her upper lip with the back of a black glove.

"It's not blizzarding," Vivian argued. "It just started to flurry. And it's not dumb to be here. It's pretty."

"Is it? I can't see anything under all the snow."

"The snow is pretty," Vivian countered.

"We could watch the snow from the hotel."

"It's not the same."

"You're right, it's better."

Vivian shot Rose a frustrated look.

"It's like going to the movies," Rose explained. "It might be totally awesome to go watch a movie about Transformers, but you don't actually want giant robots coming down, attacking the city, and killing all of us, do you?"

Vivian took another long sip, like her throat was dry.

"Snow won't immediately kill you," she argued softly.

"It might." Rose was unconvinced. If they were out here much longer, she wasn't going to make it.

When all hope seemed lost for shelter or warmth, the snow parted in front of Rose's line of sight like the Red Sea in front of Moses, and once she realized where they were in the park, she saw that they were only a few feet away from a gazebo. It was probably the oldest, frailest wooden gazebo Rose had ever seen in her life, but even though it looked more rickety than their hotel elevator, it also looked as good as the presidential suite from out in the middle of their nightmarish winter wonderland.

"Please tell me we can go sit down," she begged. "At least until the snow passes."

Rose didn't hear an immediate reply from Vivian, but she didn't hear a protest either, so she picked up her speed, boots crunching through the solid snow to claim their spots on the gazebo before someone else could take them.

Not that anyone else was around.

Rose had moved several feet before she realized that Vivian hadn't quickened her pace to remain beside her. They were close enough to the gazebo, though, that Vivian wasn't going to get lost behind her, so Rose kept marching. She wouldn't stop until—

Something hit her in the back.

At first she thought it was a dead bird that hadn't managed to fly south for the winter in time, and being pelted with fowl carcasses almost sounded better than being bombed by camouflaged bird shit the same color as the snow. Then Rose remembered the History Channel special about the Abominable Snowman that Vivian had left playing on the hotel room TV while she was in the shower, and Rose became convinced a yeti was coming after her.

If it was a yeti attacking her, though, it had a really pretty voice.

"See? Snow doesn't kill you."

When Rose turned around, all she saw behind her was Vivian and a crumbled sphere of snow, broken into powdery fragments on the ground behind her.

Vivian had hit her with a snowball.

She was actually twelve.

Rose almost wanted to play along, to feign melting like the Wicked Witch of the West, but that would require collapsing into the snow and she was pretty sure that might actually kill her.

"Stop messing around!" Rose called behind her. "This is a business trip, remember? You're on company time."

Vivian smirked the whole way to the gazebo, clearly proud of herself, and Rose couldn't tell if the confidence came from proving her point or pissing Rose off.

Probably both.

The gazebo was basically the equivalent of the straw house in the story of The Three Little Pigs, but it was better than nothing, even if the Big Bad Wolf was blowing his harsh winter breeze directly at them through the slits between the logs of wood. The structure did little to break the wind and the wooden seats inside of it were practically frozen solid, but Rose had checked her ass in the mirror before they left and she knew her backside was hot enough to warm them, and at least the gazebo blocked out enough snow that she could see more than a couple of feet in front of her.

She had a much better view of Vivian now, who slumped in the seat beside her, close enough that Rose could feel some of her body heat even through their layers of clothing. Thankfully, she had no more snowballs in hand, just her drink which she sipped from heartily. The way it seemed weightless in Vivian's palm told Rose the chocolaty liquid was almost gone.

"What are we supposed to do in here while the snow passes?" Vivian asked. "Exchange rings? Say our vows? We don't even know how long it's supposed to be snowing for."

"What happened to 'it's just a flurry?'" Rose raised a cynical eyebrow. "It should pass soon. Besides, there's all kinds of stuff we can do."

"Like what?" Vivian challenged.

"Like talk," Rose answered.

Vivian scrunched her nose, as if the thought of conversing with Rose like she had already been doing since six o'clock this morning was something she hadn't even considered. "Talk about what?"

"I don't know." Rose shrugged. "Anything. Like…you and Jana."

Vivian grimaced. "Jana? What about her?"

"You know," Rose started. "How you get along with her as a vice president. How you feel about her managing the office while you're gone. How you have her underwear in your bag."

Vivian rolled her eyes. If she wasn't in the mood for talking before, she certainly wasn't now. "She's a fine vice president, she's a fine office manager, and we've already been over her clothes."

"But have you been under her clothes?" Rose asked.

Vivian almost spit out her cocoa in surprise. "Why on earth would you think that?"

"Don't play dumb," Rose said. "You gave me the password to your laptop. I've seen your emails, *babe*."

Vivian cringed again, and Rose would bet anything Vivian was regretting bringing her along for this trip.

"Is this because of the snowball?" Vivian asked.

"Gotta get revenge somehow," Rose said. "Now give me the deets."

Vivian pulled away from a sip of cocoa like the chocolate left a bitter taste in her mouth. "Must you ask me about my personal life? Why can't we talk about, I don't know, literally anything else?"

"Because that stuff's boring. Everyone loves hot gossip about office hookups."

"How would you feel if I pestered you about stuff like that? Tell me, how's your love life going?"

"I'm painfully single," Rose revealed, effortlessly shrugging even around the bulky down shoulder pads of her jacket. "See? Not that hard to talk about, is it?"

Vivian scoffed. "You're not the only one."

"Are you sure?" Rose asked. "'Cause it sure seems like you and Jana are dating."

"We're not." Vivian was stern in her answer, channeling the bitch she'd been on their flight this morning.

Rose realized that as guarded as Vivian was, a serious discussion about her love life was probably off the table, especially when she was conversing with someone who was practically a stranger, but Rose wasn't one to abandon a juicy story when she was hot on its trail. "But you are sleeping with her, right?"

Vivian was silent.

"Wow. The president of Gio Corp. is dating her vice president. How scandalous."

"We're not dating," Vivian reiterated.

"Okay. 'President of Gio Corp. *Banging* her Vice President.' *That's* a less incriminating headline. I'm sure Gene would be happy to read that when he sat down with the Sunday paper and a bowl of Wheaties."

Rose's sarcasm wasn't winning her many brownie points, and Vivian looked like she was about to rip her a new one. Rose held her gloves up in defense.

"Relax. I'm not going to say anything. I'm not one to judge, and besides, I gave you a dildo for Christmas, remember?"

Vivian smirked momentarily like she had the upper hand, but her face quickly turned sullen. "Thank you. But it's not Gene I'm worried about."

Rose was too curious not to ask. "Who, then?"

"No one, really," Vivian said. "It's stupid. Please stop asking me questions."

"All right," Rose agreed. "I'm fine with ending the conversation with you calling yourself stupid if you are."

Rose's taunt spurred Vivian on. She knew it would.

"It's my ex, okay?" Vivian revealed. "Her name is Chelsea. We were together pretty much the entire time I was going to business school. We met in high school, we lived together, we graduated together. I thought I was going to marry her. Then she left me, completely out of the blue, for some guy in one of our entrepreneurship classes. He was a real sleazeball, too. Came from money. Thought his ideas were better than everyone else's because his great-great-grandfather invented some stupid corn-shucking device back in the 1800s. Apparently, business is in his blood, and marrying some rich, over-glorified redneck was more appealing to her than staying with her girlfriend who managed a dying office."

"He sounds like Nick," Rose noted.

Vivian scoffed, but with the way her gaze was buried in her lap, Rose could tell she was more sad than angry. "Yeah. You could say I know his type."

"How long has it been since you and Chelsea broke up?"

"A couple of years." Vivian spoke vaguely. Rose recognized the way Vivian said it, like she was pretending she didn't know the exact date, couldn't figure out the exact number of days it had been since they'd last been together after a mere moment of calculation.

"Does Jana know about her?"

Vivian nodded. "Of course."

"You are close to her, then. You don't talk about your ex to some girl you're just fucking."

"Well, apparently I do," Vivian insisted. "Because we're just fucking."

Rose knotted her brow. "Why is it so important for you to stress that? You make a big deal out of it every time I even imply that you might like Jana for more than her body."

Vivian was silent.

Rose figured it out on her own.

"You're afraid of commitment."

"I'm not afraid of anything," Vivian said. "I just know that it's probably not going to work out long term, so why let myself get attached?"

"That's stupid," Rose said. "You don't know that. Jana could end up being the next big era in your life."

"What do you know?" Vivian asked. "Your idea of dating is flirting with random flight attendants. I don't think Heather is 'the next big era' in your life."

"That's different," Rose said. "You clearly like Jana."

"Liking her is not the same as planning a life with her. The likelihood just isn't there."

"So what?" Rose said. "That doesn't mean you shouldn't try. As long as there's even a small chance, it can still happen. Hell, there's only like a one percent chance of dying in a car crash, yet my dad managed to pull that one off."

The confession slipped out on its own. Rose hadn't said it to garnish sympathy or trump Vivian's pain, but Vivian looked up at her with mournful eyes anyway. "I'm sorry."

"Don't be. It wasn't your fault." Rose was tired of pitying looks and condolences. She had gotten enough of them after the accident when it left Beth a struggling single mother raising a twelve-year-old daughter on her own.

"How did it happen?"

Rose usually didn't tell this story. It might do Vivian some good to hear it, though, just to get her mind off Chelsea. Rose sighed hard before speaking, her breath clouding her vision. "Just a car crash. Highway pileup. Some other guy died too, so I could never really be mad about it. It didn't feel right. Another family was going through the same thing we were, and I felt worse for them than I did for myself. The other guy had two kids, and they were both younger than me. Like, a lot younger. One of them was four, maybe. The sister was a bit older, but I don't think that boy is even going to remember his father. At least I got to know mine first, you know? We felt so bad that we went to their funeral. Their family came to ours, too."

Vivian seemed to think about that for a moment, probably trying to judge which of them had been through worse. Rose knew they'd both had it bad. It didn't feel right to compare her suffering to Vivian's. Rose had moved forward with her life years ago. Vivian was still stuck in the past. She needed the support. "I'm sorry about Chelsea," Rose offered, hoping a less combative route would put her back on Vivian's good side.

"I hate talking about her," Vivian admitted.

Rose nodded. "I hate talking about my dad, too. I don't usually tell people."

"You told me."

Rose shrugged. "You told me about Chelsea." She took another sip of cocoa. She was almost out, and what was left wasn't so much hot anymore as it was lukewarm. "Sorry for pestering you about Jana. It's not really my business. I figured you were so hush-hush about it because you were coworkers, not because you were hung up on someone else."

"That's all right," Vivian said. "I'd probably be curious if I were you, too." Vivian took a deep sigh and slumped back in the wooden seat as if exhausted. She looked down at the paper cup in her hand with a frown. "I need a drink."

Rose offered the last of her own cocoa. Sharing with Vivian didn't sound so bad right now. If they could swap life stories, they could swap a little spit, too.

"I mean your kind of drink," Vivian said. "I'm actually looking forward to going out tonight now."

That one sentence flipped Rose's entire mood. She reburied the emotions she'd unearthed and smiled as wickedly as she could muster. When she stood up, she grabbed Vivian's hand and pulled her up from her seat.

Vivian followed her with a sense of uncertainty, Rose's giddiness shocking her more than the tundra outside the gazebo.

It had stopped snowing, finally, and they hadn't even noticed. Rose smiled into the clear air.

"Let's go, then."

Chapter 8

"Take me to a gay bar."

Vivian stopped shaking from the cold and settled for looking shaken up. "What?"

"Don't pretend you don't know any good gay bars close by," Rose said. "It's my first time in New York. I want to see something new."

Vivian's pace seemed to slow as she thought. Rose slowed down with her, but she hoped they wouldn't be strolling along the sidewalks for much longer. They just had gotten out of the cab, but already the cold was nipping at her again, and she wanted to be inside a heated building as soon as possible.

"Do you even like girls?" Vivian asked, and Rose was taken aback by her surprise.

"Of course I like girls," Rose said. "Did you really think I was straight?"

"Well, there was the stewardess, I guess, but I thought you were joking around. Besides, your sexuality is none of my business."

"How did you not know, though?" Rose asked. "How did you think I picked up on you and Jana so quickly? Straight people can see two girls making out with each other and call them 'good pals.' I'm too observant to be heterosexual."

"I figured you were just smart," Vivian said, still dazed.

"Well, I am that, too." Rose put on her cheekiest grin, cheeks no doubt made rosier by the cold. "Can we go inside now?" she asked. "It's freezing, and I'm starving."

Vivian nodded. "I know a place."

Vivian picked up her pace and led Rose confidently around the block. Rose was happy to get her blood flowing again and figured she may as well talk to distract herself from the rest of the walk.

"So now that we've got the coming outs out of the way, how do you feel about picking up someone at the bar and taking her home?"

Vivian's signature scowl returned. "I'd prefer if you didn't."

"Come on." Rose elbowed Vivian in the side, wiggling her eyebrows. "You can watch."

"I'm not going to be the third wheel watching you and some girl hook up in our hotel room."

"Then bring someone back for yourself. If you and Jana aren't dating, that means you can sleep with whoever you want, right? If you don't care about her, let loose, have a little fun. Ever heard of, 'What happens in New York stays in New York?'"

Vivian pursed her lips, frowning slightly at Rose's challenge. "Maybe I will."

"Ok then," Rose said. "It's a deal. If we can both find dates that are cool with some weird tourist hotel room orgy, we'll bring them back. But if we don't both find dates, I'll be considerate and leave mine at the bar so I don't keep you up all night."

"You're assuming I'm the one who won't find a date?"

Rose shrugged. "I'm just saying I'm hot and have a good track record of getting hit on every time I go out."

"'Getting hit on' is too vague," Vivian said. "Little things like looks from across the bar don't always count. People can look at you because you have food in your teeth. Or an obvious alcohol problem. Phone numbers are what count."

"Yeah, if you're trying to take them out to dinner next weekend," Rose said. "I don't know about you, but when I pick someone up at a bar, I barely even remember their name. I'm not rummaging through their stuff looking for a phone number or an address I can contact them with later. Just a credit card so I can steal their identity."

Vivian's eyes widened.

"That's a joke."

"Good. After this Nick fiasco, I don't condone stealing anything."

"You're not going to steal any hearts tonight?" Rose asked, wiggling her eyebrows in a way that was probably not as alluring as she intended.

"It's not hearts I'm after," Vivian said. "We're not looking for phone numbers, remember?"

Rose smiled. She liked this side of Vivian. "Let's go, Lady Killer."

———— ⁘⁘⁘ ————

Rose didn't realize just how hungry she was until she was half a plate of nachos and a beer in. Beer wasn't usually her drink of choice, especially if she was going out with the intention of not being sober when she came back, but she needed something bitter to wash down the sweet taste of the hot chocolate and nothing went better with nachos than a nice ale.

Vivian had gone a similar route, but had opted for a burger instead of the nachos, and was already halfway through her second bottle of booze. She'd chugged the first before their food even arrived, and Rose wondered just how drunk she was trying to get tonight. A beer couldn't even get Rose tipsy, and two didn't seem to do much for Vivian either, especially with all that food fresh in her stomach to cushion the effects of the alcohol, but the night was young, and Rose wanted to stay sober enough to see Vivian cut loose.

Vivian wasn't going to get drunk on beer, though.

Rose raised a hand to flag the bartender down. Nearly everyone who worked here was cute and covered in colorful tattoos, and the bartenders were uniformed in sleeveless tanks that showed off their arms. None of the girls here were unattractive, and if her and Vivian's night went well, she would surely remember to come back here if she was ever in New York again.

A cute girl with long, brown hair and tattoos swirling around her biceps like galaxies approached them at Rose's beckon. She was cute. Nothing too impressive but not bad.

"I'm getting a martini or something," Rose said. "You want anything?"

Rose was hoping she'd say yes and order something with a bit more alcohol in it, but Vivian shook her head. "Just another beer, please."

Disappointed, Rose ordered for the both of them anyway. Maybe Vivian would want something else after seeing Rose's drink.

The bartender was speedy with their order, probably because it was still fairly early and the bar wasn't too packed yet. That was also the reason Rose hadn't done much window shopping for a one-night stand. There wasn't much of a selection to choose from when there were more staff in the room than patrons.

She was still eating, though. Maybe by the time they finished dinner the bar would fill up along with her stomach.

"We're not going to pick up a lot of chicks this way," Rose said.

"What way?" Vivian asked. Their three empty bottles were stacked in the middle of the counter between them, lined up in a perfect triangle like Vivian was going to knock them over with a greasy, balled up napkin and win Rose a stuffed animal that wouldn't fit in her luggage on the way home.

"All we've done is eat and talk to each other," Rose said, sipping on her drink, taste buds adjusting to the change of flavor. "We can't pick up girls if we don't interact with them. The only woman we've even looked at all night is the bartender."

As if 'Bartender' was her name and this was some kind of cocktail party, the woman behind the counter who'd been serving the two of them appeared again, this time friendlier than when they'd first arrived. She laid a tattooed arm against the counter as if she was going to stay for a while.

"You guys need anything else? You want another martini?" she asked Rose, looking at the almost half-empty glass in her hand.

"No, thanks," Rose said. "I'm taking things a little slow."

"I haven't seen you two here before," the woman continued.

"We're just visiting," Vivian said. "It's her first time in New York." She pointed at Rose.

"That's cool," the bartender said. She was lying. Rose could only imagine how many tourists she'd had to listen to as they told their stories of just how much they loved The Big Apple. "Are you two a couple?"

Vivian practically choked on her burger. Rose laughed.

"No, we work together." Rose said. "We flew in from DC for a business meeting. She's the president, I'm the vice president."

Vivian side-eyed Rose for telling their story that way, but she was too busy hacking beef out of her lungs to speak up and correct her.

"How long are you in town for?" the bartender asked.

Vivian finally managed to clear her throat, but her face was still red, either from choking or the embarrassment of being mistaken for a couple with Rose.

Rose jumped in again. "'Bout a week," she said, swirling the straw around in her drink with nimble fingers. The plastic clinked against the sides of the glass, effectively drawing the bartender's attention to Rose's graceful fingers, exactly where Rose wanted her to look.

She watched Rose pop an olive in her mouth seductively before speaking again. "Well, feel free to stop by any time. Don't be shy. And if you need anything else, just call for me. I'm Echo, by the way."

"Echo?" Vivian asked when the bartender danced away from their section of the counter. "That's a fake name if I've ever heard one."

"Duh it's a fake name," Rose said. "How many creepy, clingy drunk people do you think hit on her every night? She doesn't need everyone knowing her real name. Besides, Echo sounds like a fun name to scream out in bed. Repeatedly."

"She's not going to sleep with you," Vivian said a little too defensively. She didn't sound confident, and Rose used that to her advantage.

"You don't know that. She was totally flirting with me."

"Please." Vivian rolled her eyes. "She lives on tips. She has to flirt with all of her customers if she wants to pay the rent. She probably thinks you're another one of those creepy patrons you were talking about."

"If she thought one of us was creepy, it was you," Rose said, scooping up the last remaining puddle of cheese with an unbroken tortilla chip. "You're the one that barely talked to her at all. It's always the quiet ones that are the secret serial killers."

"Whatever. She was here for like five seconds. And you hijacked my conversation. I have just as much of a chance with that girl as you."

"In your dreams, maybe. I even gave you the higher title and she was still more into me. Point Joe Biden. Sorry, Barack. The vice president comes out on top this time."

"She wouldn't be so into you if I told her you were just an assistant," Vivian threatened.

"I see how you're playing," Rose said. "You know I'm better than you, so you have to tear me down just to put yourself on top. Those are dirty tactics right there, Ms. Tracey. You might as well call yourself a Republican."

"That's politics." Vivian shrugged. "And business. It's cutthroat."

Rose scoffed. "I can get women more easily than you any day."

"You're on," Vivian said. "Forget finding dates. First to seduce the bartender wins."

"Challenge accepted."

Rose threw back a swig of her drink like it was a shot and slammed her forearms onto the sticky bar counter with conviction. When Echo came back around, she made sure to get the first word in.

Rose gestured to her empty glass. "Can I have another drink?"

"That was fast."

"What can I say? Some things just go down easy."

Rose winked and caught a glimpse of Vivian rolling her eyes in her peripheral vision. She was so distracted she barely noticed Echo's reaction. Her voice wasn't as chipper as Rose remembered from earlier when she said, "I'll get you another."

Echo busied herself pouring the drink, and Vivian took the opportunity to scold Rose while she was out of earshot. "Oh, yeah, show her how fast you can get drunk. Super appealing."

"Like you've got a better pickup line."

"Watch this."

In the time it took for Echo to make the drink, another group of girls had sat at the opposite end of the bar. When Echo strolled back over with Rose's martini, it was clear she had her sights set on serving her new patrons, but that didn't stop Vivian from stalling her.

"I like your tattoos."

Vivian couldn't have picked a worse time to say a stupider pick-up line. Echo's previously bare bicep was now covered by a rag she'd slung over her shoulder. Vivian's sudden compliment was so unexpected that she had to pull the rag away to take a look at the markings herself to see what had warranted the comment. The design was a typical complex tribal pattern. Nothing exceptional enough to work as a conversation starter.

"That blue is the same color as your eyes."

Was that tattoo even blue? Rose couldn't tell in the dim, strobed lighting of the bar. The ink looked brown from where Rose was, but so did Echo's eyes, so maybe Vivian wasn't entirely wrong.

"Thanks." Echo accepted the compliment almost as awkwardly as Vivian had given it. She tried to make a break for it, but Vivian stopped her again.

"Do you live around here?" she asked.

Echo's eyebrows lurched defensively, like a threatened cat rising on its toes. Vivian was so quick to backtrack she stammered out her explanation. "I just figured you'd know the sights," she said. "Is there anything here we should check out?" Vivian tried to recover by not-so-subtly raking her gaze across Echo's figure, showing Echo just how interested she was in checking things out.

That was Echo's final straw.

"Look," she started, losing the smile she'd obviously forced onto herself at the beginning of her shift. "This is going to have to stop." Her eyes shifted between Vivian and Rose, and Rose was on the edge of her seat as soon as she realized she was being included in the backlash of Vivian's fuck-up. "I can tell that you two are hitting on me, all right, and I can also tell that you're not business women. Business professionals? They don't act like this." She pointed an accusatory finger at both of them, swirling it around like the two of them were a drink she was mixing. "I'm not even sure why you're hitting on me, because I can tell that you two are a couple. You've only been here an hour and all you've done is argue like you're married. Hell, you probably are married. I won't judge you for what you like to do in bed, but I'm making it clear right now that I'm not interested in swinging with you. I won't kick you out yet, but if either of you needs anything else, please ask a different bartender."

Both of them were speechless.

Rose was pretty sure Echo had ripped out her vocal chords while she was busy ripping Vivian a second asshole. As soon as she found them again, the first words off her tongue were, "*What the fuck?*"

Vivian started laughing. Like, full blown wheezing guffaws, and Rose couldn't tell if it was a nervous habit or if she genuinely found this funny.

Because it *was* kind of hilarious.

Okay, they kind of deserved it, especially Vivian. Echo wasn't entirely wrong in telling them off, but the married couple thing? Definitely worthy of a few guffaws. Rose hadn't heard anybody so wrong since an hour ago when Vivian thought she was straight.

Maybe it was the alcohol she'd chugged, or maybe Vivian's laughter was as contagious as Echo's stupidity, but Rose joined her in throwing her head back and letting loose.

Their chorus was loud enough to attract some attention in the still fairly empty room, and as both of them tried to quiet down, all Rose could think about was how Vivian was right. Sometimes girls didn't stare from across the bar because they thought someone was cute. Sometimes they stared because two girls were laughing like they were way more drunk than they actually were.

The two of them didn't really calm down until another woman appeared behind the bar, one who looked more like Echo's boss than her coworker. She began cleaning the countertop and rummaging the bar for drinks to pour, but she never took her eyes off Vivian and Rose for more than ten seconds. It was more than obvious that they were being watched. Echo had clearly ratted them out to one of her supervisors.

"You're going to get us kicked out," Rose said through clenched teeth. She leaned in close to Vivian in order to keep her voice down, afraid so much as another peep would get them thrown out onto the street.

Vivian leaned in even closer to her, even more careful than Rose. "I didn't do anything," she said.

"There's no way you're that bad at picking up women. You pissed off that bartender on purpose."

"I didn't. She was crazy! Did you hear her? What would I possibly have to gain from making her mad?"

Rose took another calming sip of her drink and subtly eyed the manager over the glass to see if she was still watching them. She was.

"I think you scared that bartender away so you didn't have to sleep with her," Rose whispered, setting her glass down to look Vivian in the eye. "You don't want to find somebody else to replace Jana. Or Chelsea."

"That doesn't even make sense."

"It does. That was the most pathetic thing I've ever seen. You *have* to have more game than that. You had a girlfriend for fuck's sake. And you have Jana! How could you possibly manage to get either one of them if you have no idea how to talk to women? You did that on purpose."

"Now you're just drunk," Vivian said.

"Now you're in denial," Rose said. "You care about Jana and you don't want to mess up what you have with her. I *know* that's what you're doing, whether you want to admit it or not."

"I don't care about her like that," Vivian said.

"Replace her, then."

"Fine." Vivian leaned forward until there was almost no space between her and Rose, until her whispers were so quiet Rose could hear the open and close of her mouth more clearly than the sounds of her words themselves. Her breath was hot, sour, and Rose couldn't tell if the liquor she smelled was wafting from her own lips or Vivian's.

"What are you doing?" Rose asked, a lump suddenly in her throat. The way her head swam made her feel much more drunk than she had thirty seconds ago. Unless Echo had spiked her last drink, Rose wasn't sure she could blame the alcohol.

"You're my vice president replacement aren't you?" Vivian asked, teasing Rose with the false moniker she'd given herself. "So replace my vice president."

The kiss caught Rose by surprise, but the press of her lips against Vivian's wasn't as surprising as how much Rose liked it.

Vivian tasted like ketchup and beer, like the smells of her childhood and the thrills of being an adult all wrapped up into one. She was spicy and bitter and salty and sweet and the way Vivian threaded her hands into the hair at the back of Rose's head and pushed her forward made Rose want to fall off the bar stool to bring the two of them even closer, to tumble head over snow boots into Vivian's lap.

The kiss only ended when she very nearly did just that. Vivian was the only thing that saved her from falling off the bar stool and twisting her ankle on the legs of her seat. Her hands were around Rose's waist in no time, catching her and stabilizing her until Rose was able to center herself on the chair again and make the move for the second kiss of her own accord.

Rose was pretty sure she was the one who introduced tongue to the kiss.

That was probably the best decision she'd made all night.

If Vivian's lips were satin-soft, her tongue was velvet, and the way she licked inside Rose's mouth, cradling her jaw to hold her in place, made Rose breathless.

This was why Vivian had Jana. This was why she was going to marry Chelsea. Maybe the girl had no game, but damn could she kiss when she scored.

She'd have to apologize to Vivian later for insulting her.

Or just keep kissing her and never stop to do something as useless as speak with her mouth ever again.

There were other things her mouth could be doing.

A lot of other things.

Things Rose shouldn't do in public in front of a bartender she'd just tried to convince she wasn't dating Vivian.

Making out in plain sight wasn't helping their case, and it only served to give Echo more ground, but if the rest of her weird, political role-play fantasies came true, too, maybe that wouldn't be so bad.

Rose was going to be the president though, vice president replacement or not.

Rose owned her kiss, and the more Rose gave, the more Vivian took until Rose could barely remember that Vivian was the one who had initiated the kiss in the first place.

Rose couldn't remember a lot of things right now. Her mind was elsewhere, and that was only partially the alcohol's fault.

Somehow, when Vivian pulled away to tilt her head and adjust the kiss, Rose mustered up the clarity to put a hand against her chest and push the two of them apart, just far enough that their lips couldn't meet even if they both stretched. And, God, did Rose want to stretch for it.

Vivian looked upset, like she was afraid she might have done something wrong, but Rose soothed her worries faster than a few bottles of beer could.

"Do you want to get out of here?"

The way Echo was looking at them from across the bar made it feel like they didn't have a choice. The manager was getting closer now, too, and when Vivian said, "Yes," Rose breathed a sigh of relief.

The manager was a big, burly woman who looked better suited for the position of a bouncer than a bartender, and she stalked Rose and Vivian like she was going to pick them up by the scruff of their necks, one in each muscular hand, and throw them out onto the snowy pavement. She leaned in so close to them from across the bar that Rose could read the word *Queen* written in nearly illegible cursive across her forearm.

Not even singing "We Will Rock You" could save them now. It was more like "Under Pressure." Or "Another One Bites the Dust."

"I think you two should go," Queen said gruffly, eyeing the two of them like she was going to beat them up for their lunch money if they didn't pay the tab soon. Vivian dug around frantically in her wallet as if she was looking for a get-out-of-jail-free card, but she settled for laying her debit card on the counter instead.

Queen snatched it from the bar like she wasn't going to give it back and shuffled to the register.

"I can pay for mine," Rose said, anxiously thumbing through the folds of her wallet. Vivian put a hand on her arm to stop her.

"It's no big deal," Vivian said. "It'll be faster if we let her charge the whole tab on me."

Rose nodded and slipped her wallet back into her pocket.

Queen was back in a flash, tossing Vivian's debit card at her like it was a dart and the bull's-eye was her face. As the two of them stood to leave, Queen saw them off with a gracious, "Don't come back!"

A warning Rose planned to heed.

Chapter 9

"I KNEW YOU WERE GOING to get us kicked out," Rose said.

The night was colder now than it had been earlier, and Rose made a show of putting on her gloves to protect her fingers from the chill. When she looked to Vivian, she wasn't doing the same. She'd left her gloves on the counter.

Rose wasn't going back in for them.

It seemed Vivian wasn't either.

She didn't seem to mind the cold too much anyway. Between getting each other hot and bothered with that kiss and the fire Queen had lit under their asses, the cold was almost welcome.

It was sort of funny, really, and when Rose finally pulled her gloves on and met Vivian's gaze, they both burst into another fit of laughter.

"I still don't think it was my fault," Vivian said.

"First you pissed off Echo and then you kissed me," Rose said. "Totally your fault. I hope you're using this time to think about what you've done wrong."

"Are you asking me if I regret kissing you?" Vivian asked. "Because I don't."

Rose bit her lip. "No?"

"Nope." Vivian smiled shyly. "I liked it."

"Me, too."

Vivian shoved her hands in the pockets of her jacket, more to give herself something to do than to actually keep them warm. She bounced on the balls of her heels for a moment before looking back to Rose like a teenager about to ask her date to prom. "Want to kiss some more?"

Rose's smile wasn't as innocent as Vivian's. "I thought you'd never ask."

Rose was the one who pushed up on her toes to initiate the kiss this time, snatching Vivian's lips with her own to warm them in the cold night air. It was instinctual, easier than most kisses Rose shared with strangers outside of bar entrances, and as soon as their lips met, the awkwardness faded. Vivian's hands were on her cheeks, and she was kissing Rose with all the confidence she'd had the first time she'd done it inside the bar.

When Vivian's tongue swiped across her bottom lip and pried her way inside Rose's mouth, a pit of fire that formed in her stomach warmed her entire body better than any cup of hot chocolate ever could.

"You're a really good kisser," Rose said between nips to Vivian's bottom lip.

"I'm good at other things, too," Vivian said, mimicking Rose and pulling her in close by the waist. The way their pelvises bumped into each other was not coincidental.

Rose hummed happily. "Mm, are you? That's some big talk. Maybe you should show me instead."

"What wrong with a little dirty talk?" Vivian asked, showing off with another deep kiss. "It makes for great foreplay. And everyone knows foreplay is the best part."

"It's only foreplay if you actually get to have sex afterwards," Rose said, moving her hands from Vivian's hips to wrap them around her neck. "Which we're never going to be able to do if you don't call a cab and get us back to the hotel."

"There's an alley behind the bar."

Rose hoped that was a joke.

"As sanitary as that sounds, I think I'll take my chances with the grimy hotel mattress. Thinking of all the old men who have ordered pay-per-view porn and jacked off on it really turns me on."

"Ugh," Vivian groaned. "This is not making me want to go back to the hotel any faster."

"Take me to the hotel, or I'll fuck myself in the shower later and leave you to masturbate to shitty hotel porn alone."

"Fine," Vivian said. "But if you do end up fucking yourself in the shower at some point this week, please call me into the bathroom so I can join you."

"Deal."

Vivian wasn't much taller than Rose, but the way she extended her arm into the air to hail a cab made Rose feel like Vivian was towering over her. She felt small as she huddled into Vivian's side, waiting for the acknowledging honk of a car willing to pick up the both of them.

They didn't have to wait long. What cab driver in his mid-thirties didn't want to pick up two drunk young women late at night?

Rose went against her better judgment and climbed in the back of the taxi anyway. If anything happened, she and Vivian could fight him off. If he didn't pull anything, though, there were plenty of other things Rose and Vivian could do in the cab to occupy themselves.

The driver was friendly enough for someone clearly begrudgingly working the night shift, and he listened intently as Vivian fed him the address of their hotel. He seemed even more pleased when Vivian said her final words to him.

"Take the long way there."

The driver shifted gears with a smile on his face at the prospect of putting a few extra bucks in his pocket for a speedy trip he wouldn't normally make much off, and Vivian sunk into the backseat with a wicked grin like she knew she had Rose trapped.

Rose was ready to order the driver to take a short cut and threaten Vivian with the promise of locking the bathroom door next time she showered, specifically so Vivian couldn't join her, but then Vivian's mouth was on hers again and Rose forgot why she would ever want to sabotage a chance to sleep with her boss.

The cab was small and fit for no more than two people, but Vivian somehow managed to turn the tiny backseat into a space fit for three. Rose took the seat behind the driver, and Vivian wedged herself into the middle seat of the bench close to Rose.

She leaned down, pressed a kiss to the corner of Rose's mouth and unfurled Rose's scarf until it lay around the back of her neck like an undone tie. Her right hand snaked around the column of Rose's throat and then they were kissing again.

Vivian didn't stop until Rose's throat vibrated against her hand with a gentle moan and Rose pulled away, breathless.

"I can't believe we wasted the entire day not kissing," Rose said. "We could have been kissing for, like, the last sixteen hours." She accentuated her claim with another brief kiss. This time Vivian pulled away.

"I don't really think Gene or Nick would have appreciated us making out all through the meeting," Vivian said, swooping down for another peck.

"Who?" Rose asked, then realized where she was and why she was here. "Oh, right. Sorry, my job is the last thing on my mind right now."

Vivian snaked a hand in between Rose's thighs, fingers climbing the denim on Rose's knee. "There's a certain job on my mind right now," she teased, a smile overtaking her face like a weed.

Rose raised an eyebrow and lowered her voice. "You really want to give me a hand job in the back of a taxi?" she whispered, trying to spare the cab driver's ears even though he had probably heard worse in his time.

"I would if I could," Vivian said, toying with the fabric barring her hand from Rose's skin. "Next time wear a skirt."

"Do you want my pussy to get frostbite?"

"No, the biting comes later." She slipped Rose's scarf further across her shoulder and nipped lightly at her collarbone.

Rose placed a gloved hand over Vivian's bare one at her thigh, both to have something to hold on to and to make sure Vivian wouldn't move. Vivian threaded her fingers into Rose's.

"You left your gloves at the bar," Rose said. "Your hands are going to get cold."

Vivian's hand snaked even further down Rose's thigh, dragging Rose's hand with hers until they both stopped at the seam of her jeans. "Don't worry, I know where else to put them to keep them warm."

The heel of Vivian's palm pressed against her center, and Rose was really starting to regret not wearing a skirt.

Frostbite might be worth it.

It was that kind of thought that made Rose realize that things were going very far very fast, and if she didn't take care of business now, her head was never going to be clear enough to do it later.

She placed her free hand against Vivian's chest and pushed her far enough away that they could have a face to face conversation.

"Ok, before this gets to the point of no return *in the back of a cab*, I need to know how drunk you are."

"I've been drunker," Vivian said.

"That also means you've been more sober," Rose said.

"I'm not that drunk."

"That sounds suspiciously like what drunk people say when they're not sober enough to give consent but still want to get laid."

"I want to have sex with you," Vivian said, trying her hardest to sound as sober as possible. She was doing pretty well, but Rose still had to be sure.

"Drunk you wants to have sex with me."

"Sober me wants to, too."

Rose lifted another eyebrow. "Really?"

Vivian shrugged. "You're hot. And that whole bitch thing does it for me."

"Excuse me?" Rose asked, wondering if she'd heard that right.

"You're a bitch," Vivian said pointedly, looking Rose in the eye. "I'm into it, though."

Ok, Rose *was* kind of a bitch. She wasn't dense enough to deny that. If anyone other than Vivian had said that to her while she was sober, she probably wouldn't have accepted the insult without defending herself. But here with Vivian so close to her and her mind clouded by alcohol and the admission that the girl she was making out with now had thought about sleeping with her while she was sober, too, Rose was too flattered to care.

She didn't push Vivian away again when she leaned in for another kiss, this time one more gentle and controlled.

Rose hadn't forgotten about the hand between her legs, though. She tried not to make her squirming too obvious.

"You're sure you want to do this?" she asked finally, giving Vivian one last chance at a way out. "I don't want you to regret it in the morning."

"I won't," she promised. "I want to do this." Rose could feel the genuineness in the way Vivian kissed her, and when she pulled back and whispered, "You're not too drunk are you?" Rose knew Vivian's head was in the right place.

"No, I'm good," she assured.

"You sure?" Vivian asked. "'Cause that sounds suspiciously like what drunk people say when they're not sober enough to give consent but still wanna—"

"Shut up and kiss me."

Vivian met Rose's demand with a smile.

There was no gentleness anymore, no innocence in the way Vivian chewed her bottom lip then soothed the wound with her tongue, and there was nothing PG about the way Vivian's hand found the button on her jeans. She managed to unhook the metal with a skilled thumb and lock her fingers around the zipper beneath it before Rose squeezed her hand with her own, signaling her to stop and glancing nervously toward the rear view mirror at the front of the cab where she stared back at herself, eyes dilated and glossy, pupils so big she could barely tell her eyes were blue beneath all the black.

Vivian followed her line of sight until she saw what Rose was looking at. She held Rose's gaze in the mirror as she spoke to her. "He's seen worse," Vivian said, fiddling with the zipper, but not pulling it down without Rose's consent. "He's watching the road anyway. He doesn't care."

Rose bit her lip exactly where Vivian had. The skin was so raw that it nearly burst beneath her teeth. "We can't," she said regrettably. "I'm not into strange men watching women finger me in public. Besides, what happened to 'foreplay is the best part?' Save it for the hotel. Move your hand."

Vivian obeyed, letting the zipper fall slack, but she tested Rose's boundaries by moving her hand up toward her coat, grazing her side until her fingers traveled up the center of Rose's chest where Rose separated their hands to let Vivian move on her own. The zipper on Rose's pants might have been off limits, but Rose made no protests when Vivian tugged the zipper of her jacket down to her waist and slipped a hand beneath the open flap of the material, stroking a hand along Rose's breasts.

Rose never took her eyes off the mirror. It was painfully obvious what they were doing, but at least the flaps of her coat disguised Vivian's hand and left something to the imagination. The cab driver couldn't see how stiff her nipples were, how they indented the cups of her bra so far that they poked out from behind the fabric of her shirt, too. He couldn't see the way Vivian rolled them between her fingers, pinching them in a way that made them stand out even more than the cold.

It was hard for Rose not to whimper. When Vivian abandoned one breast, an act cringe-worthy on its own, to pay attention to the other, Rose was pretty sure she let out a fairly solid moan. It was hard to tell, though. Her head was foggier than the cab windows beside them, and she couldn't hear anything besides Vivian breathing heavily into her ear as she kissed the sensitive skin beneath it.

Thank God the cab driver was playing music.

He could probably still hear them, though.

Rose was starting to care less and less.

Somehow it had gone unnoticed to Rose that Vivian was popping the buttons on her shirt, too, threading the plastic spheres through their hoops as expertly as she had on her jeans, until she saw in the mirror a flash of her own skin, a small, pale expanse across the middle of her chest just big enough for Vivian to slip her hand inside her shirt and fondle her outside her bra.

"You're wearing far too many clothes." Vivian punished Rose by chewing lightly on the lobe of her ear.

Who knew Rose Walsh had a biting fetish?

Rose Walsh didn't.

She was starting to regret telling Vivian to move her hands away from her crotch. Now she had nothing to grind against, and it was more than pathetic to watch herself squirm against the seat.

Vivian couldn't take her eyes off the gentle rocking of Rose's hips. "I can't wait to taste you," she confided, giving an extra hard squeeze to Rose's breast. Her other hand was tense on her own knee, clearly restrained from touching something. What she wished she were doing with it, Rose could only imagine.

But maybe Vivian didn't have to waste her time imagining, too.

Rose waited for the right moment, until the driver was preoccupied turning a corner and watching for oncoming traffic, to tug a glove off one of her hands and stick it briefly down her pants.

Because of the undone button, she was met with little resistance. She worked her way inside her underwear easily, ignoring how wet they already were and diving directly into the source of their dampness, pressing a finger flat against her center to coat it in the same liquid ruining her panties.

Drenched, she quickly pulled away before the driver had a chance to catch her, sliding that same finger over her clit on her way out. She needed as much temporary relief as she could get.

Vivian stared at Rose's lap in a daze. She hadn't blinked in minutes, but when Rose brought her fingers to Vivian's lips, Vivian's eyes closed in ecstasy and she sucked the juices from Rose's digits as if she was parched.

Much to Rose's dismay, Vivian's hand slipped out of her shirt to snake around her waist and grip harshly around her hip. Vivian was squirming even more than Rose now, and she wasn't quiet about the way she moaned around Rose's fingers or released them with a loud pop after she sucked them clean.

The way Vivian greedily licked her lips told Rose she tasted good, but she got to experience the flavor for herself when Vivian crashed their lips together again. She kissed so hard Rose was sure it would bruise. She welcomed it, though, eagerly savoring the heady taste of herself on Vivian's tongue. They kissed long after all the traces of Rose's cum had vanished from Vivian's lips, Vivian's hand never straying from her side and Rose's uncovered hand making its way toward Vivian's lap, resting in the same position Vivian's hand had against her thigh earlier.

They easily lost track of time that way, neither of them separating to clear the fog from the windows and see what part of town they were in. It was the driver that told them the car had stopped. He coughed heartily until the two of them looked his way. How long he'd been watching or sitting there letting the meter run, neither of them knew.

"Wanna go for another spin around the block?" Vivian asked, and Rose almost thought she was being serious until she chuckled and extricated herself from Rose's grip, reaching into her pocket for her wallet to pay the driver while Rose busied herself buttoning her shirt.

She held her second glove with her gloved hand, determined not to leave it in the cab like Vivian had left hers at the bar but unwilling to contaminate them with the hand that had been in Vivian's mouth and down her own pants. Vivian wasn't as hesitant to avoid the same hand. She grabbed it as she opened the door and stepped out of the cab, helping Rose out with her.

The cab driver abandoned them in the parking lot, hand in hand under the dim glow of still-lit rooms shining from the windows stories above them. Vivian held Rose's hand as they rushed inside, escaping the cold with the billowing puffs of their breaths flowing behind them like the exhaust of an engine.

The clerk who greeted them from the front desk now was a new one, a pregnant woman who'd relieved the teenage boy from earlier. Midnight graced her with dark circles beneath her eyes, but Rose didn't feel anywhere near as tired.

"Stairs or elevator?" Vivian asked.

"Elevator," Rose said, giving Vivian's hand a firm squeeze. "I want to make out in it."

"Stairs are faster," Vivian said, leaning down to kiss Rose and give her a preview of what she would be missing out on if they wasted time in the elevator. "I kind of want to get to the room as soon as possible."

Rose pressed her lips together, savoring the taste of Vivian and deciding whether she could be bribed with kisses or not.

She could.

"I can't believe I'm saying this, but you're right. The stairs are better in this case."

Satisfied, Vivian wasted no time in climbing them, pulling Rose behind her on the steps until they reached the second level of the building and the door to their room not too far from it. Her hands were shaky when she pulled the key card out of her pocket, either from excitement or the alcohol or some combination of the two. Still, she managed to unlock the door on the second swipe, and Rose wasted no time barreling into the room behind her and shutting the door by shoving Vivian up against it and attacking her with another kiss.

Vivian immediately went for Rose's clothes, slipping her hands into the shoulder pads of Rose's jacket and stripping it from her arms before pulling off her own coat, too. The fact that they were standing by the coat rack held little meaning for Vivian as she threw their clothes to the ground haphazardly, shuffling around them as she attempted to walk Rose closer to the beds. She didn't make it far before Rose slammed her into the wall again.

"Oh, no. You had your fun in the cab. You don't get to tease me all night and not expect a little revenge."

Vivian swallowed hard, and Rose kissed her throat where it bobbed.

"Undress me," Rose said.

Vivian was quick to listen, undoing the buttons on Rose's shirt for the second time that night and finally pulling the zipper of her jeans down where Rose hadn't let her before. Rose had tugged her second glove and scarf off and kicked her shoes and socks from her feet at the same time Vivian did when they entered the room, and Vivian had no trouble sliding Rose's shirt down her arms or her pants down her thighs until Rose was in nothing but her underwear before her.

Vivian was staring, enraptured by the sight of Rose's body, and Rose utilized her stunned state to undo the top few buttons of Vivian's shirt, opening it enough that Rose could see cleavage and the tops of the cups of a silky black bra through the slit, which she stared at almost as intently as Vivian stared at her.

"You just gonna stand there?" Rose asked, her half-naked body pressed against Vivian's fully clothed one against the wall. She stepped away a couple of feet, turned around, and lifted her hair to unveil her back and leave Vivian with room to work. "You going to take this bra off me or do I have to do it myself?"

Rose was wearing the bra Vivian had lent to her, the one that actually belonged to Jana, and Vivian tugged at the clasps and freed them almost before Rose could finish her sentence. Impressed, she watched as Vivian slipped the material off her body and dropped Jana's bra to the floor like she no doubt had a dozen times before.

"You were pretty quick at that," Rose said, turning around to face Vivian bare-chested. Vivian focused more on her breasts than making eye contact as they spoke. "How many times have you taken that bra off Jana before?"

"A few," Vivian said, reaching out to cup a hand over one of Rose's breasts, breath hitching as her thumb circled gently around a goose-bumped nipple.

Rose leaned into the touch, pawing briefly at Vivian's own chest over her clothes before tugging Vivian away from the wall by her belt loops over to the first bed she could reach. It happened to be Vivian's.

The covers on Vivian's bed were still immaculately pressed, tucked in, and unwrinkled. Rose laid Vivian on them gently, head settling in against the pillow before Rose straddled her waist and leaned down to capture her mouth in another kiss.

Rose's hands found Vivian's and guided them down her body, bypassing the sides of her breasts and her rib cage, down to her hips and finally to the elastic band of her underwear where Vivian picked up on what she was supposed to do. She pulled Rose's underwear down by her thumbs, digits grazing the curve of Rose's ass and the back of her thighs on the way down. With some resituating, the underwear met the floor with the rest of Rose's wardrobe, and Rose was fully naked above Vivian, who ran her hands over Rose's chest again, coaxing her to scoot up farther onto the mattress to allow Vivian to suck one of her nipples gently into her mouth.

Rose moaned, balancing herself on the mattress with one hand and cradling Vivian's head against her chest with the other, guiding her to one nipple and then the other with her hand threaded in Vivian's dark curls. When Vivian reached a hand lower, stroking Rose's stomach and trailing down to the top of her mound, Rose stopped her by lifting herself up.

"You want to taste me, don't you?" she asked, to which Vivian nodded fervently, eyes glossy and dark. That was all Rose needed to scoot farther up the mattress until her hands rested against the top of the headboard and her sex was directly above Vivian's face, legs straddled around her head.

Vivian didn't hesitate to place her hands on Rose's lower back, slip them down to cup the cheeks of her ass, and lift her head the rest of the way to meet Rose's center. Her tongue threaded hungrily through Rose's folds, lapping at the juices around her clit and labia. She sucked happily, swirling her tongue in small circles around the bud while it was in her mouth, then releasing it to lick large ovals across the area around it without touching her most sensitive areas directly.

It wasn't long before Rose was squirming like she had been in the cab, letting her body relax and her hips sink down onto Vivian's face until she was practically grinding against the woman beneath her. Vivian allowed Rose to buck her hips against her mouth, Rose doing half the work as Vivian's tongue slid up and down her slit, caressing her clit in figure eight patterns interrupted by the occasional gentle suck of her lips and the even rarer careful graze of her teeth. Eyes open, Vivian watched as Rose's chest heaved above her, breasts swaying slightly with each jerk of her hips.

"Inside," Rose said, and Vivian listened too carefully. As her tongue trailed lower, dipped inside the entrance of Rose's center, her hand snaked down between her own legs, desperate to copy the actions of her tongue on Rose with her fingers on herself, but Rose felt the hand move away from where it had been grabbing her ass, and she searched for it with her own until she found it. Vivian had only managed to unbutton and unzip her jeans before Rose trapped her hand back beside her head with her own.

"Wait your turn."

Vivian whimpered like a dog, and it took everything in her for Rose not to say, "*Who's the bitch now?*"

Rose got off on watching Vivian struggle to contain herself beneath her. Between the cab, the wall, and right now, she could only imagine how wet Vivian was, how soaked Rose would find her when she finally let Vivian experience what she was feeling now. She tried to contain her orgasm, prolong it for as long as she could to make Vivian suffer, but it was hard when she couldn't control her hips, and was constantly taken aback by the way Vivian expertly used her tongue to fuck her, filling her until Rose ground against the muscle lapping at the ridges inside of her like this was the last time she would ever be able to sit on somebody's face. As soon as Vivian's tongue met her G-spot, nails carving small half-moons into her ass, Rose was done for, spasming above Vivian and gripping the headboard with caution, like she might break the wooden plate if she held onto it with the same amount of force she felt as her orgasm ripped through her.

Collapsing onto the sheets beside Vivian, breathing heavily as she tried to calm her heart rate, Rose couldn't remember the last time she'd felt so good after sex. If any of her exes had made her feel that way, it was a distant memory that dangled just out of her reach, and when Rose turned her head toward Vivian, the sight of her mouth, cheeks drenched in Rose's cum, was an erotic vision unrivaled by any fantasy or hook up she'd ever had before. Rose kissed her full force, tasting herself on Vivian's lips much more powerfully than she had before. Vivian was salty, yet somehow still sweet, and Rose could probably kiss her forever.

Vivian needed a lot more than that, though.

"Please," she begged, trying hard not to sound desperate but failing as she tried harder to abide by Rose's rules. She was high-strung, impatient, but doing everything she could to convince Rose it was time for her turn.

Rose didn't need to hear any more.

Once again she climbed atop Vivian, this time laying their bodies flush together as she continued to kiss the woman beneath her, placing kisses from her lips down to her jawline and her neck, then back up again to lick the wetness from the contours of her mouth. Her hands traveled lower, undoing the rest of the buttons of Vivian's top until she was able to take it off, Vivian maneuvering a hand behind her back to undo her bra with slightly more difficulty than she had Rose's. Soon Vivian was topless beneath her and Rose ran a hand over one petite breast, feeling the nipple perk beneath the palm of her hand as her other hand traveled lower, slipped inside Vivian's jeans where she had already undone them.

Vivian sighed with delight as soon as the tip of Rose's middle finger grazed her clit, her ring and index finger soon taking their place beside it to stroke Vivian in broad, heavy circles that stimulated her almost more than she could take. She hissed in pleasure, digging her fingernails into Rose's arm as it continued its movements, working Vivian's own juices around the sensitive nerves.

Vivian wrapped her legs around Rose's waist to give her fingers easier access, and Rose took advantage of that, plunging all three of her fingers slowly into Vivian's cunt, waiting for the muscles to accept her, adjust to the pressure of the new addition, before pumping her fingers in and out, increasing her pace the wetter Vivian became.

The wet slap of skin on skin filled the room along with Vivian's moans, and Rose didn't care if they were waking up the neighbors.

"I'm gonna…" Vivian whimpered around shouts of Rose's name, and Rose curled her fingers up, let Vivian's muscles tighten around her as she whispered into Vivian's ear, "Cum for me."

Vivian did, clenching around Rose's fingers in a fierce wave of pulses as her abs tightened under Rose's and her body tensed with the buildup of release.

When Vivian stopped panting and gathered enough breath to sloppily kiss Rose again, Rose withdrew her fingers, bringing them to her lips and admiring the glossy sheen leaking its way across her knuckles and down to the head of her palm. Vivian's eyes were still dilated, wide and satisfied, and when Rose slipped a finger into her mouth, Vivian accepted it without hesitation. When Vivian licked her clean, Rose slipped the other two fingers into her own mouth, finally getting her first taste of the other woman. Her eyes closed as she hummed happily and savored the flavor.

"You taste…almost as good as me," Rose said, and even laughing felt better than usual in their post-orgasmic bliss.

"That's a lie and you know it," Vivian said, but instead of arguing her own delectability as Rose thought she was going to, she said, "You taste much better than me."

"I'll take the compliment," Rose said, "But you definitely don't taste bad." Rose chewed her bottom lip, glancing between her shining fingers and Vivian's naked body. "Can I clean you up?" she asked, and Vivian nodded, propping herself up on her elbows to give herself a better view of Rose sliding down her body, settling between her legs.

Rose made quick work of the rest of Vivian's clothes, sliding her jeans and her underwear down in a single motion and exposing Vivian's sex to the air. She looked even wetter than she had felt, and Rose used the moment it took to remove Vivian's pants from around her ankles to admire the sight in front of her. As soon as Vivian was naked, Rose dove in.

She hadn't gone down here with the intention of going down on Vivian, but the way Vivian moaned when her tongue swiped across the expanse of her skin told Rose she was still sensitive and enjoying this as much as Rose had enjoyed Vivian's mouth on her. She looked up, met Vivian's eyes, and waited for the nod that signaled round two.

With Vivian's juices coating her tongue, Rose had all the lubrication she needed to pay special attention to Vivian's clit, timing the sweeps of her tongue across the bud with its own subtle twitching. The faster Rose licked, the more Vivian moaned, and it was probably a given that the whole floor could hear them by now. The last thing Rose needed was the hotel staff barging in with a noise complaint, so she picked up her pace, assaulted Vivian with quick flicks of her tongue until she was falling over the edge again, cumming, and soaking Rose's face with her juices.

Rose did her best to clean Vivian up quickly as she fell from her high. Vivian looked exhausted in the best way possible, and Rose didn't think she or the rest of the floor could withstand a round three. She closed Vivian's thighs, working her way back up the mattress until her head rested on the pillow opposite Vivian's. Vivian cleaned the cum off Rose's face with another kiss.

"Do you want me to move beds?" Vivian asked, sighing in content and collapsing against the mattress like she might pass out at any moment.

"We're in your bed," Rose said, gracing Vivian's cheek with another lazy kiss. "I'd be the one to move."

"Oh." Vivian hummed, then added, "You don't have to."

"Do you want me to?" Rose asked.

Vivian shook her head.

"Then I'll stay," Rose said, settling herself against Vivian's side and tugging the comforter out from where it was tucked in at the corner of the mattress. Vivian did the same and they both climbed under the covers, cocooning themselves in the sheets to get comfortable. "Big spoon or little spoon?" Rose asked, and Vivian looked relieved that she was the one to ask.

"I'm taller," Vivian said. "Big spoon."

"Fine with me."

Rose found it surprisingly comfortable to lie that way, Vivian's arm wrapped around her midriff and her breasts pressing against the line of her back. She was warm, soft, and before long Rose noticed her eyelids drooping, lulling her into sleep.

"Fuck."

"Hmm?"

"You wanna get up to turn the lights off?" Rose asked.

"No," she admitted.

"Me either," Rose said. Dying sounded better than moving at this point. Vivian felt too safe to move away from. "I can sleep with them on," she said.

"Me too," Vivian mumbled sleepily. "Not my electric bill."

Rose laughed. Vivian smiled against her shoulder blade, giving it one final feather-light kiss.

"Goodnight, Rose."

"Goodnight, Vivian."

They fell asleep illuminated by the glow of the fluorescent bulb above them and the streetlights of New York all around them. When the sun rose from its grave along the horizon, neither of them could be bothered to care.

Chapter 10

When Rose woke it was bright. Not, "aliens have abducted me and—wait, what's that feeling in my ass?" bright, but bright like "why the fuck didn't I turn off the lights last night?" bright.

And then Rose remembered why.

Vivian was still curled into her side, hands wrapped around her waist and hair tangled with Rose's against their pillows.

She was also naked.

Yeah, that was why.

She remembered everything—the bar, the kiss, the sex, the not wanting to get up and turn off the light switch because Vivian was warm and soft and *naked* next to her and they were both tired from all the sex.

All the *great* sex.

Rose didn't regret a minute of it and hoped Vivian felt the same way, but it wouldn't surprise her if her boss and bed companion experienced a morning-after freak. They'd been drinking last night. Not a lot, but not a little either, and because Vivian was fun when she was tipsy didn't mean she wasn't going to revert back to her old stuck-up self the morning after.

Maybe she wouldn't remember? Maybe she'd be angry and think Rose coerced her while she was in a drunken state?

If Rose could manage to slip out of bed without Vivian noticing…

A kiss on the lips hit her like a smack to the face. Rose was so blindsided by it that she could only let instinct take over, pucker her lips and kiss back until Vivian pulled away, leaving her wide-eyed and stunned.

Apparently, Vivian was fun the morning after, too. She had a nice glow about her, brighter than the hotel room lights or the sunshine filtering through the window.

Yeah, she definitely didn't regret last night.

"Do you always kiss the girls the morning after?" Rose asked.

Vivian shrugged. "If they're as cute as I remember them from the night before."

"So you think I'm cute?"

Vivian chewed her bottom lip and smiled down at Rose from where she was propped up on her side. "You're not bad."

"Whatever." Rose rolled her eyes. "I'm hot and you know it."

"Didn't say you weren't."

Rose hummed in contentment. "Your hangover isn't too bad, is it?" she asked, concerned.

"Don't have one."

"Really?"

"I told you I wasn't drunk last night."

"No, I guess you weren't." Rose was relieved. This morning was not going the way she expected it to, and Rose liked this alternative much better.

"How's your hangover?" Vivian asked, an equal amount of worry in her voice.

"I wasn't drunk either."

It wasn't a lie, but she hadn't exactly been sober. Her skull was pounding a little, but the headache plaguing her could just as likely have been the result of sleeping with all the lights on. Or a symptom of caffeine withdrawal.

"Do you want coffee?" Rose asked, noticing the scratchy fuzziness of her tongue. She hoped her mouth hadn't been too gross when Vivian kissed her. She guessed not by the way Vivian kissed her again.

"Yes. I'll get it." Vivian pulled the sheets off of her and stood, leaving Rose lonely and cold.

Rose was glad she didn't have to do the work. She'd had a pretty big day yesterday.

A first class upgrade flight, a secret mission into Vivian's office, a walk in Central Park, and a night of much more fun than Rose had expected to have for the entire trip. All within twenty-four hours.

She'd had worse days.

Wistfully, she watched as Vivian brewed instant coffee at the kitchen counter. It was difficult to decide which was the more heavenly— her first cup of morning coffee or a naked Vivian serving it. Definitely the two complemented each other, she thought, and she didn't want to be without either.

Vivian set the cups carefully on the bedside table, leaning down to kiss Rose as she made her delivery.

"You're in a kissy mood this morning," Rose said as Vivian settled back into the sheets beside her.

"I like kissing you," she said.

"I like kissing you, too."

"Then there's no problem, is there?"

"I guess not."

If Vivian hadn't gotten a big whiff of her morning breath before, she did now as she pressed their faces together as close as they could possibly get, kissing Rose like her mouth was uncharted territory her tongue was destined to explore. It wasn't lustful, per se, but it wasn't sweet either, more like a promise of more to come. They separated only when their coffee had cooled.

Rose blew the dying steam away from her cup like a gnat at a picnic, and prayed for steady hands. Her wish was granted. Something about Vivian soothed her. Rose felt relaxed, not frantic like she typically was when she woke up in a stranger's bed after a one-night stand. Maybe it was because Vivian's room was Rose's room too and all of her luggage was only ten feet away. Maybe it was just because she'd known Vivian longer than three hours before she had sex with her.

Maybe it was just because Vivian was a good kisser. Whatever it was, Rose appreciated it.

For the first time in a long time, when Rose took a sip of her coffee it did almost nothing for her. No rushing sense of euphoria, no sudden rejuvenation. She tried to blame that on the weakness of the coffee rather than the fact that waking up next to Vivian had already left her feeling refreshed.

"I hope you don't mind it black," Vivian said. "I couldn't find any cream."

"I don't need cream. But I'd appreciate it if you gave me a little sugar."

Rose swept in for a kiss, this time taking Vivian by surprise. Her coffee sloshed gently in her cup.

"That was a terrible pickup line."

"I don't need to pick you up," Rose said. "I've already got you naked in my bed."

"My bed."

"Holiday Inn's bed."

"Touché."

"You know what touché translates to, right?" Rose asked.

"Touch," Vivian said simply.

Rose pouted. "Boo. You're not supposed to know the answer."

"Sorry, I took advantage of the incredibly rare opportunity of taking French classes in public high school. Didn't mean to outshine your brilliance." Vivian's sarcasm was so palpable Rose could almost touch it.

No pun intended.

"I was going to teach you by touching you, but you ruined the moment. Don't you know girls are supposed to be dumb? Nobody wants to sleep with a woman who expresses her intelligence."

"Is that why I wanted to sleep with you last night?" Vivian asked.

Rose was more impressed with Vivian's wit than offended by the insult. "Your tongue is scathing."

"You'd know all about my tongue, wouldn't you?"

Some incredibly wonderful flashbacks from the night before told Rose that she did indeed have much experience with Vivian's tongue.

There was always more to learn, though.

"A little." Rose blew harder on her coffee, trying not to burn her own tongue. She had plans for it later. When she took another sip, it was good.

Probably not as good as Vivian, though.

She licked her lips, recalling the memory.

Vivian watched her, her look curious, then changing to serious. "How do you feel?" she asked, and Rose knew she wasn't asking about the coffee.

"I feel…good," Rose said, stretching her legs beneath the sheets and beaming at Vivian, hoping her own face glowed as much as the girl's beside her.

"That's an understatement," Vivian agreed.

"It definitely is, but how would you know?" Rose spoke. "You're the one getting laid regularly. At least, I'm assuming you are if you have that not-girlfriend of yours over to your apartment enough that she leaves her underwear there."

Rose glanced at the floor, failing to locate Jana's bra after Vivian had ripped it off of her last night. Their clothes were a jumbled mess, and Rose couldn't sort through any of it just by sight alone. Oh well. She wasn't getting up. The bra wasn't hers, and she wasn't going to miss it. It wasn't like she planned to put clothes on anytime soon.

"I haven't had sex in months," Rose said.

"I guess that means we have to make up for lost time."

"I guess it does."

"So do you want to do this?" Vivian asked, tone hopeful, and Rose knew what she meant.

Rose nodded. "I do. I had fun last night. I want it to happen again. But maybe without all the alcohol and the whole pissing off the bartender part. There's only so many gay clubs we can get kicked out of before we run out of bars to go to." Vivian chuckled and Rose turned serious again. "Are you okay with sleeping together again?"

"I'm cool with having a fuck buddy for a week," Vivian said honestly.

"Just a week?" Rose asked.

Vivian shrugged. "I don't know. When we get back to DC, we won't work together for much longer, and I don't imagine I'll see you around town much. Plus, you live with your mom, so..."

Rose cringed. "God, that makes me sound so uncool."

"It is kind of uncool," Vivian said, laughing a little.

"When did you move out?" Rose asked, suddenly realizing that as little as Vivian knew about her, she knew even less about Vivian. All she knew was that Vivian had been working for Gio Corp. since she was eighteen, her last girlfriend had broken up with her, and she was great with her tongue. She should get to know Vivian if they were going to be friends, even if it was just friends with benefits.

"Sixteen," Vivian said, and Rose tried not to choke on her coffee.

"That's a little early, isn't it?"

Vivian shrugged. "I guess."

"Did you have shitty parents or something?"

"Not really," Vivian said. "We were kinda poor, I guess, but I just wanted to go off and do my own thing, support myself. I got a job, finished high school, then joined Gio and took a bunch of classes to get my business degree. I graduated early so I could start getting promotions and actually make a decent living for once. Six years later, I was the president."

"You're smart," Rose said, as if Vivian didn't know it.

"Of course," she said. "I took a whole year of French classes, remember?"

Rose laughed. "I took Spanish."

"Me too. I quit French once I realized Spanish would look better on a job application. When do you get your degree?"

"I still have another semester." Rose groaned.

"That's another reason we probably can't keep this up when we get back," Vivian said. "You'll be busy with classes."

"Classes aren't very hard for me," Rose said. "I'm good at what I

Shaya Crabtree

do. It doesn't take a lot out of me, so you can take me out any time you want."

Vivian chuckled. "Nice one."

"Thanks, I'll be here all week."

Vivian smiled, then kissed her. "And maybe more than a week. We'll see what we can work out back in DC. But for the love of God, please stop with the bad jokes or we're not even going to make it to Friday."

"I'm sure there's plenty we can do to keep my mouth preoccupied so that doesn't happen." Rose placed her empty cup back on the nightstand. Vivian did the same.

Rose found herself sinking into the sheets as Vivian pushed her down, positioning her upper half halfway on top of Rose. Their breasts collided as Vivian's arm snaked around Rose's head and she bent down for a kiss. Rose was prepared this time, not like the first kiss that morning that had taken her by surprise, and not like the clumsy kiss they'd shared after Vivian made them coffee. This one was more passionate, more sensual, and Rose stopped it before it went too far.

"Do you want to take this make-out session to the bathroom?" she asked. "We could shower together. Also, I really need to brush my teeth. I'm sure my breath smells terrible."

"Your breath smells good," Vivian said, and Rose raised an eyebrow skeptically.

"Vivian Tracey, president of Gio Corp., likes the smell of ass breath." Rose announced the news to an imaginary crowd of people, channeling her inner town crier or some asshole who ran an inaccurate celebrity gossip blog online.

Vivian smacked her cheek playfully. "It doesn't smell like ass," she said. "Does my breath smell bad?"

Rose thought for a moment. "No," she said honestly.

"Then you must like ass breath, too."

Rose laughed before running her hands down Vivian's back and slapping her ass playfully. "Toothpaste breath smells better, though. Let's go."

The hotel room was probably colder than New England winters and their DC office combined. As soon as Rose shucked the sheets to meet the air and bury her toes in the frozen padding of the carpet, she regretted it immediately. Until she saw the way Vivian's body was reacting to the temperature. Her skin prickled and nipples tightened. Cold was good. Rose could deal with cold. She was going to hell for the thoughts she was having about Vivian's body anyway, so she'd appreciate the chill as long as she could before she was damned to spend the rest of eternity in hellfire. And judging by the way Vivian's eyes never left Rose's chest it was clear Vivian was going to be taking that same trip with her.

That was another vacation Rose looked forward to taking with Vivian.

The bathroom was even colder than the rest of the room, carpet replaced with tile and the light bulbs cool with lack of use. Rose started the shower before she even made her way to the sink, absorbing the steam of the hot water and relishing in the way her shivers subsided. Vivian looked thankful, but her nipples didn't seem to get the memo. They stood at attention, and Rose wondered if that was from the cold or the excitement of what was to come.

Vivian was already in front of the mirror, toothpaste in hand and toothbrush out of its holder on the counter. Rose grabbed her own and stood beside Vivian, bumping elbows with her as they attempted to share the small space and stare at each other in the mirror. With all the toothpaste foaming around her lips, Vivian looked like a rabid dog, and Rose would have made some comment about her being a bitch if her own mouth wasn't full of bristles and she didn't get sidetracked cursing herself for not washing off her mascara last night before she went to bed. Her makeup looked like a train wreck, and it was a wonder Vivian had even wanted to kiss her this morning.

The President of Gio Corp. DC is into ass breath and clowns.

"Better?" Vivian asked as Rose rinsed her mouth and dried her face with one of the small, over-starched towels.

Rose ran her tongue over her lips, moistening them. "I don't know, you tell me."

Their next kiss was minty fresh, potent with peppermint, but laced with the bitter aftertaste of coffee. Rose pulled Vivian in by her hips, their pelvises colliding and nipples grazing as the kiss deepened into a swirl of tongues.

"This is the part where I'd take your clothes off if you were wearing any," Vivian said, separating their lips momentarily for air.

"Being naked saves time. It's efficient."

Vivian's hands grazed Rose's side down to the jut of her hip, leaving a trail of goose bumps in their wake. "I do love efficiency."

"Then thank me for already having the shower started, too."

"Thank you."

When Rose turned to slide back the shower curtain and step into the tub, she could feel Vivian's eyes burning into her ass even hotter than the steam, and the enticing sway of her hips as she moved was totally intentional.

The shower was small, meaning the two of them wouldn't have fit in the tub if they'd tried to take a bath together, but standing they had enough elbow room to move around as they wished—not that Vivian let any space come between them. Rose stood directly under the stream, letting the water soak her hair, while Vivian wrapped her arms around her from behind, her hands settling against Rose's stomach and breasts pressing against her back. The edges of the spray misted her as she pressed their bodies together, kissing the side of Rose's neck.

"Sex first or shower first?" Vivian asked. Her hands found their way to the top of Rose's mound, fingertips ruffling the thin patch of hair growing there.

"Sex," Rose said, closing her eyes and leaning into Vivian's touch.

If they were going to get dirty, they might as well do it before they got clean.

"As you wish."

Vivian led Rose out of the stream and pressed her face-forward against the wall where the coldness of the tile made Rose's nipples harden even stiffer than they already were. Vivian pushed herself up against Rose's backside, leveling Rose's ass with her center, and her hands found their way up Rose's chest, tweaking her nipples easily with the added wetness of the water and appreciating the way the sensation made Rose moan and buck her ass against Vivian's thighs.

She suckled Rose's neck, licking the water from her skin and leaving a light bruise in its place. Rose made no protests, only tilted her head to give Vivian more room. She'd have a mark later, but it was winter. She could cover it up with a scarf. Everything felt too good for her to tell Vivian to stop.

"Does that shower head come off?" Rose asked, breathless.

Vivian looked up to examine the device. Rose hated every second Vivian's lips weren't on her. "No."

"Fuck," Rose said. "Mine comes off at home. It's...convenient."

Vivian shuddered against her. "It turns me on to think about you touching yourself," she said.

"Really?" Rose teased. "Because it gets boring touching myself day after day after day after..."

"Shit," Vivian muttered, and Rose knew she had her boss right where she wanted her.

"I'll just have to have someone else touch me for a change." Rose laced their hands together like she had in the cab, guiding Vivian's hand away from her breasts, down her abs, and to where the shower head would be if it were removable.

Her fingers dipped into the liquid pooling between Rose's thighs, and Rose subtly widened her stance to give Vivian more room.

"More." Rose groaned.

Vivian kept her movements painfully slow, stroking Rose's clit where it was most sensitive.

"I swear to God if you don't fuck me properly I'm going to do it myself."

She sped up her movements, rubbing Rose's clit sore before trailing her hand down, testing the wetness of her entrance with the tip of her middle finger and plunging in, slowly at first to allow Rose to adjust to the pressure.

"More," Rose moaned again, and Vivian picked up her pace, massaging the inside of Rose's walls before adding a second finger and exploring her fully, pumping in and out and hitting Rose's G-spot with each stroke.

Rose placed her hands against the wall in an attempt to balance herself, but the harder Vivian fucked her, the less stable she became. Her fingers curled along with her toes, gripping uselessly at the flat tile. Soon Vivian had to anchor them both against the wall as she rubbed her clit against Rose's ass. The grinding was natural, and as long as Vivian never stopped fucking her, Rose would let Vivian get off any way she wanted to.

Two fingers going to town on her was more than enough for Rose, and she could feel her abs tighten and her stomach warm with longing. Vivian grinding against her ass and kissing along her throat helped her orgasm wash over her like the cascade of water from the showerhead.

As her body relaxed, Rose could still feel Vivian tense behind her, still holding her up and still rocking gently against her backside. Rose pulled away from the wall and pushed Vivian off of her, earning a whimper of disapproval that Rose was happy to hear. She was going to make Vivian pay a little for making her wait so long to get off. She turned around to kiss her on the lips.

"You're much better at that than my showerhead."

"I'm sure your showerhead would be very impressed with me," Vivian said, her voice gruff with lust. Rose was going to prolong the conversation for as long as possible.

"Impressed with your skills? Maybe. Impressed with your totally lame dry humping? Not so much."

Vivian's face settled into a slight frown which Rose wiped off of her with another kiss.

"We're in the shower," Vivian said. "Is anything dry?"

Rose stepped forward carefully, inching her way into Vivian's space on the slippery tub until Vivian had her back pressed against the wall.

"Certainly not you," Rose said and tucked a hand between Vivian's thighs to cup her mound. Heat radiated off of her, and Rose watched Vivian's eyes roll back as her fingers spread her lips.

"Please."

"Please what?" Rose asked.

"Move. Anything."

Rose obliged by twirling her fingers in a circular motion. She had barely picked up a rhythm when she felt Vivian bucking into her.

"I'm not going to last long."

It wasn't a lie. Vivian's breath was already ragged, and her hips were grinding in an uneven rhythm as she struggled to keep herself together. As much of a tease as Rose was, there was too much beauty in the sight before her to torture Vivian longer than necessary. Rose was desperate to see her cum, make Vivian feel as good as Vivian had made her. Denying Vivian her orgasm would hurt Rose, too. She quickened her pace.

"Fuck." Vivian's curses were almost as hot as her whimpers and only spurred Rose's motions. The sound of the running water became background noise as she focused solely on listening to the subtle changes in Vivian's moans. Rose knew exactly when she was going to cum. Not even the intensity surprised her. When Vivian's orgasm hit, Rose couldn't help but smirk.

Watching Vivian orgasm was good, but the look on Vivian's face when she came to was priceless. "Sorry." She blushed becomingly. "I know I came fast, I was just really worked up, and—"

Rose cut her off with a kiss.

"Don't apologize. That was hot. Now," she said, grabbing Vivian's shampoo from the shelf and holding it out. "Wash my hair for me?"

"This stuff smells so good," Rose lamented, closing her eyes and enjoying the way Vivian's fingers massaged her scalp.

"I know. That's why I got it for you."

"You mean that's why I got it for *you*," Rose said.

"No," Vivian said. "I mean you did, but I was your Secret Santa, too. I just didn't want to tell you that after you so kindly gave me a dildo in return. I didn't believe you when you said you'd gotten me a real gift."

The pieces were adding up in Rose's mind. "So, that's why you thought I'd re-gifted the shampoo?" Vivian nodded. Rose shook her head in defeat. "What are the chances?"

"That we drew each other for the Secret Santa or that we got each other the same gift?" Vivian asked.

Rose rinsed her hair under the stream, then plopped a dollop of the soap into her own hands to thread through Vivian's thick curls. "Both."

"It was an amusing coincidence."

"That's no coincidence," Rose said. "That right there is fate."

"Fate?" Vivian asked. The question left more room for comment, but with Rose's hands kneading into her scalp, Vivian didn't quite seem capable of philosophizing the otherworldly. Rose did it for her.

"Sometimes the universe just wants you to have an affair with your boss, you know? Who am I to protest the world's greater plan?"

That earned a laugh from Vivian, and Rose helped rinse the suds from her curls before spreading her body wash elsewhere, scrubbing Vivian from head to toe and lingering selfishly between her legs where she needed the most attention. Vivian returned the favor, soaping Rose up until she was spotless and gathering them both towels from the rack while Rose rinsed herself and twisted the shower knobs to *Off*.

They took turns drying each other before rushing to get dressed to avoid the chill. Rose almost considered taking another shower just to be warm again, but then Vivian was standing in front of her in another pair of ass-fitting jeans, and Rose didn't want to be anywhere but right here in the middle of her freezing hotel room ever again.

Vivian ruined the moment.

"I have to call Jana."

"About?"

"You."

Rose raised an eyebrow.

"We may not be dating, but I can't just sleep with someone else and not tell her. It's not classy. Plus, I left her in charge of the office. I have to check in."

"All right." Rose was fine with that, and she had plenty to do to preoccupy herself while Vivian was busy with her call. "You do that, and I'll go down to the bar in the lobby and dig through those files."

"Sounds like a plan."

While Vivian reached for her phone, Rose gathered her laptop and slipped away downstairs. The crowd in the lounge was sizable enough to provide a bit of background noise, but not loud enough distract her. The breakfast bar was the perfect spot to work. She grabbed a muffin for breakfast, sat at an empty table, opened the laptop, and typed in Vivian's password.

Now that Rose had the full financial records for the last six years at her fingertips, she knew exactly what she was looking for. Inconsistencies, peculiar patterns, and singular anomalies.

The budget distribution was clearly organized into tiers, with the bigger offices in the larger cities obviously allocated more funds. New York had the lion's share, hardly surprising considering it was headquarters. The numbers here seemed perfectly in line with what she would expect.

San Francisco, Tampa, Baltimore, and all of the other major US cities were in the B tier and all had similar budgets to each other. The South American branches had their own category, C tier, and were on the lowest budgets. Here Rose found her first clue.

DC had a South American budget, despite being in the B tier. There was such a disparity that there was no way this could be an accidental oversight. It had gone on for too long. Someone was definitely squeezing DC, and squeezing it specifically. It wasn't hard for Rose to figure out who. And then she found another anomaly.

One branch had much more money than its tier standing deserved. Rose smiled with satisfaction when she saw who ran it.

She couldn't wait to tell Vivian what she'd found. She was ready to race back into the hotel room with her findings, but she didn't know if Vivian was off the phone yet and thought it might be best to give her a bit more privacy before barging in.

She called Phoebe instead.

"Rose." Phoebe answered the phone abruptly without so much as a hello. "Do you know what time it is?"

"Uh." Rose took a guess. "Like, one o'clock?"

"Exactly," Phoebe spat out.

"Is there a problem with that?" Rose asked. If Phoebe was still asleep at one in the afternoon, Rose was going to have to arrange an intervention. That was too late, even by Rose's standards.

"Yeah. I'm at work."

"You work on Sunday?" Rose asked, incredulous.

"Where do you think I work? Chick-fil-A?"

"I never worked on a Sunday," Rose said.

"You also never work any other day."

"Ha ha."

"Just saying," Phoebe said. "Now do you need something or are you just putting my job in jeopardy to brag about the New York night life?"

"I slept with Vivian."

"Whoa." Phoebe wasn't even trying to be quiet now. Her mood did a complete one-eighty. "Tell me everything."

"There's not much to tell." She wasn't going to keep anything from Phoebe— Rose trusted her not to get Vivian in trouble and spill the secret to anyone else (besides Harley maybe)—but there really wasn't much to disclose yet. "We got tipsy last night and ended up in bed together." And in a cab. And in the shower. She left that out. Phoebe didn't need all the dirty details.

"Is she good?" Phoebe asked. "Are you going to sleep with her again?"

"Already did," Rose said. "I guess we kind of have this 'friends with benefits' thing going on. At least until the trip is over."

"You're unbelievable," Phoebe said. "You give a dildo to your boss, end up going on vacation with her to New York instead of being punished, and then get to have sex with her, too? Only you could pull that off, Walsh."

"What can I say, fate likes me."

"Did you sleep with fate like you slept with your boss?"

"No. I bet Vivian's better in bed than fate anyway. Also, fate would never fuck me…over."

"I'm so jealous."

"What? No exciting happenings going on at the office to brag about?" Rose asked.

"No." Rose could sense Phoebe's pout through the phone. "Everything's boring since you left. I don't even have a cell-mate, er, *cube*mate. Harley tried to move in with me, but she can't because she's a technician and apparently there's a line in company policy about cross-department cubicle sharing being the eighth sign of the apocalypse."

"That sounds awful." Rose offered a bit of sympathy, but quickly moved on to heckling Phoebe about her relationship. "So, you and Harley are ready to move in together?"

"Yep," Phoebe said confidently. "We flew to Vegas yesterday. Got married. Now we're expecting."

"You mean *she's* expecting," Rose said, assuming by Phoebe's brag that Harley was the one carrying their imaginary child.

"No," Phoebe said. "We got each other pregnant. We're gonna have twins. Kinda."

"Man, you go to New York for two days and you miss everything." Rose huffed.

Phoebe went quiet for a moment, then spoke to Rose in an urgent whisper. "Hey, I gotta go. Jana's glaring at me over the cubicle. I'm not supposed to be on the phone." Her voice picked up, friendly and animatronic, and Rose barely recognized her best friend as she continued talking. "Thank you for your cooperation. We value our customers here at Gio Corp. and if you have any further questions, please don't hesitate to call again. However, I hope your problem is resolved because—Ok she's gone but seriously don't call me again, Rose. I'm gonna get fired." She whispered the last part, cautious, and Rose was smart enough to listen. She wasn't going to let Phoebe lose her job, too. She was here in New York to save it.

"Bye, Phoebe."

"Bye, Rose."

Rose hung up and checked the time. 1:20. If Jana was monitoring the floor, Vivian was probably off the phone with her. When Rose slipped back through their hotel room door, Vivian was sitting at the desk texting or checking her email.

"How did Jana take it?" It wasn't her business to ask, but Rose was curious for some reason.

Vivian sighed. "Not great."

Rose was afraid of that. Just because Vivian was convinced there wasn't anything emotional between her and Jana didn't mean that Jana felt the same way about what they had going on.

"She didn't actually say much," Vivian said. "But I could tell she wasn't happy. I probably shouldn't have called her while she was at work."

"Do you want good news?" Rose asked, hoping to cheer Vivian up.

"Please." Vivian set her phone down and looked up to Rose with hopeful eyes.

"I found all the missing money."

Vivian stood up slowly. "Where is it?"

"Boston."

Chapter 11

"ALL WE HAVE TO DO is tell Gene."

"That's not going to work." Rose was emphatic.

With the help of her reflection in the elevator's metal doors, Vivian adjusted the collar of her suit. "Why not?"

"Because I'm not sure yet exactly how he's done it, and Nick is going to cover his tracks as soon as we open our mouths. He'll make something up, and Gene will believe him because he's his son."

The elevator beeped. The icon of the next floor lit up.

"Slimy bastard. I can't believe he's gotten away with this for so long."

Rose could feel Vivian's rage radiating off of her, and while she understood where Vivian was coming from, she didn't understand where Nick was.

"Why did he target us anyway?" Rose asked. "There's got to be a reason he shafted DC rather than someone else."

Vivian was quiet for a moment. She stared at her reflection blankly. "Do you remember when he hit on you?"

"I'm trying to forget that, actually."

"Well, he did the same to me the first time I met him. Then he flipped out when I told him I was a lesbian. He's hated me ever since."

Rose shouldn't have been surprised that a guy like Nick was homophobic on top of being generally skeezy. It made her feel worse for Vivian.

"I have a plan," Rose said. "One that will convince Gene for good."

That caught Vivian's attention. She turned to Rose with a spark of curiosity in her eyes. "What is it?"

"Don't worry about it. Go meet Gene and pretend everything is normal. I got this."

Vivian took a deep breath then nodded slowly. When the elevator doors slid open, they both stepped into the New York office cautiously. "I hope you know what you're doing."

"I do."

They split up. Vivian made her way to the conference room as Rose made her way to Vivian's office. She set up shop at Vivian's desktop immediately. She had to work fast. Today was payday, and DC was done not getting the funds it deserved.

She easily hacked into the background programs and was surprised to see a sub program running alongside the normal payday code—a sub program that for a few hours on this one day of the month reclassified DC's tier point from B to C, the South American budget stream. The remaining funds not allocated to DC were swept over into Boston's account. *That's how he did it! Ratbag.*

She had until the noon deadline to tweak this little bit of inane chicanery or the embezzling was never going to end. Luckily, this was White Hat 101 for Rose. Nick was clever but she was a genius.

She was just about to finish when an error message popped up. The desktop beeped at her, then shut off. She was used to faulty equipment in DC, but here in New York it was suspicious. She rebooted and typed in Vivian's password, but was met with a different error message. She tried again, typing the letters in more carefully this time. No luck.

Someone had locked her out.

She had a good idea who.

If this was part of Nick's plan, all she could do was sit and wait, or, more accurately, sit back and relax. He had stopped her, but he hadn't stopped her in time. She pulled out her phone, waiting for

Vivian to text her that the meeting was over or for Nick to call her and brag about how clever he was for shutting her out.

She hadn't expected Nick to barge in to the office.

He was fuming. The door slammed open, and Rose jumped a little from the surprise of it. She almost dropped her phone, but tightened her grip on it afterwards.

Rose wasn't glad to see him, but she wasn't terrified either. "Jesus, Nick. Learn to knock."

"I know what you're doing."

Nick wasn't wasting time. That didn't mean Rose couldn't. "Okay, you caught me." Rose turned her phone around to show Nick the screen. "I'm playing solitaire on the job."

Nick's face was so red that Rose could imagine the steam erupting from his ears. She thought about turning on the phone's camera just to give him a glimpse of how ridiculous he looked, but he paid the screen no mind. He was looking dead at Rose, the veins of his eyes almost as red as the flush of his neck.

"Was it worth it?" he asked.

Rose played dumb. "Not really. This app kind of sucks. The desktop version is worth playing, but *someone* locked me out."

"Wait till Gene finds out what you did." Nick's bark was supposed to be threatening, but Rose had nothing to worry about. Not when what Nick was doing was far worse than her snooping in the name of good.

"He won't be that mad at me. Old people love solitaire."

"I don't think he's a fan."

"What about you? You seem pretty comfortable risking solitary confinement in prison for embezzling funds."

Nick smirked. "You've got nothing. One of your own men betrayed you. All tracks to Boston are covered, all the evidence is gone, and you can't prove a thing."

One of their own? As far as Rose was aware, only she and Vivian knew anything about Nick's plans. Rose didn't know what he meant, but she wasn't worried. She had something better against Nick than a double-crossing inside man. Only she knew what she'd really been doing in Vivian's office. Nick might be able to cover his own tracks, but he wouldn't be able to cover hers.

"Come on." He grabbed her arm, and Rose was so shocked by his audacity that she didn't have the presence of mind to shrug him off. "We're going to that meeting, and you're going to tell Gene what you've been up to."

Rose allowed herself to be led out of Vivian's office and down the hall to the conference room. She could hear the whisper of some of the office workers as they poked their heads above their cubicle walls. She could only imagine how shocking the sight of the CEO's son manhandling a strange woman in broad daylight was for them. She'd be spooked, too.

Okay, so this part wasn't going exactly according to plan.

Rose's stomach was a little more than uneasy when Nick burst through the conference room doors. He threw her into the room like a grenade, but Rose was glad he had let go of her all the same.

Gene didn't look happy.

Vivian looked wide-eyed and terrified.

"What's the meaning of this?" Gene asked. He stood at the head of the conference room. A whiteboard full of red writing was his backdrop.

"Sorry to interrupt," Nick said, "But guess who I caught snooping around?" It wasn't a question or an apology, but a brag, like Rose was a feral animal that'd been harassing an innocent village for weeks and had finally been tracked down and killed.

"What do you mean snooping?" Gene asked. "Nick, I can't deal with this right now. We're in the middle of a meeting."

"And I'm in the middle of stopping this woman from compromising our company. I caught her snooping around on the servers, trying to alter the pay schedule."

Gene's attitude shifted from annoyance to genuine shock. He gave Nick his undivided attention.

Rose took it back from him.

"If you're trying to say I stole money, I didn't. You sure have, though," Rose said in an attempt to turn the tables.

"That's ridiculous." Nick scoffed. "I don't manage company finances. My concerns are Boston and Boston alone."

That was the most honest thing Nick had ever said. He only cared about himself.

Rose looked Gene dead in the eye. "I didn't steal anything. You can check the numbers. I have nothing to hide."

"She didn't steal anything because I stopped her," Nick said. "I shut down her access before she could do anything."

Gene looked back and forth between the two of them. His silence voiced uncertainty, and Nick did everything in his power to sway his father to his side.

"She's a con artist!" Nick said. "Both of them are." He looked pointedly toward Vivian. "And not only are they responsible for this stunt, but I know for a fact that the two of them are romantically involved, which, as you know, is strictly against company policy. But even worse than dating your coworkers is promoting them unjustly. Do you know what Rose's job was last week?" He looked to Gene. "Data entry! Vivian promoted her just at the start of this trip so they could come here together and take extra money for themselves."

Vivian shot Rose a glance that was almost as searing as Nick's was when he barged in on her in Vivian's office.

Gene looked back and forth between the both of them. His mouth was ever-so-slightly open in shock, and Rose watched him bite down on his tongue as he stood.

"Is this true?" Gene asked.

Rose swallowed. She didn't have to lie about the financials, she didn't have to lie about Nick's embezzling, and she shouldn't have to lie about this. She and Vivian weren't romantically involved, were they? Sexually, yes. But romantically? Technically, they weren't, and Rose should've had an easy time denying it.

So why did it feel like lying?

"No, sir."

Vivian was little help. She was still stunned and stuck to her chair like a life raft.

Rose couldn't read Gene. His face, previously so gentle and welcoming, was now hardened. Rose had never seen him this serious, and she couldn't tell whether or not he believed her.

After the theft accusation, though, whether or not Rose was dating a coworker probably wasn't his primary concern.

Nick looked ready for a decision to be made right then and there. He was as eagerly awaiting his father's input as Rose was dreading it.

"This is ridiculous," Gene finally said. "I don't know what's going on here, but I can't have employees hacking my system. That's completely unacceptable. Regardless of what you were trying to do or what you would have done if my son hadn't stopped you, I'm not going to let this go unpunished."

"She needs to be fired," Nick said. "Both of them do."

"Vivian has nothing to do with this," Rose said to Gene. "She's been in here with you the whole time."

"She's covering for her because they're sleeping together."

"Where's your proof of this?" Vivian asked. It was the first time Vivian had spoken, and Rose was glad to have a second voice on her side.

Nick's scar twisted into a smile. "Jana Smith. DC's vice president. She told me everything."

Oh. Fuck.

Rose hadn't considered that Nick would find out about the two of them, and she really hadn't considered that Jana would rat them out. This entire conversation would have gone so much more smoothly without her interference. Rose and Vivian's relationship was the only real thing Nick had over them.

So much for denying any romantic connection between her and Vivian. This was an act of pure revenge.

Gene stated the obvious. "We're going to have to talk about this."

"I'd be more than happy to tell you everything." Nick claimed first word, and Gene accepted the stakes.

"Ms. Tracey, I assume you understand that we're going to have to postpone the rest of our meeting?"

"Or cancel it entirely because she'll be fired by the end of the day."

Gene raised a hand to quiet him. "We'll see about that." He looked toward Rose and Vivian. "You two stay here while I have a little chat with my son. You might want to spend your time thinking of an explanation before I return."

Gene's quiet frustration was the direct opposite of Vivian's. As soon as he shut the door behind him, she was pacing like it was locked and the key thrown away.

"This is great." She sighed.

Rose calmly sunk into Gene's chair at the head of the table. The leather was a comfortable fit, and Gene's wisdom seemed to seep into her through the material as she tried to craft her plan. "Don't worry. We can deny the relationship. There's no proof. We can say that Jana is jealous you became the president instead of her and is looking for a way to take your position. Worst comes to worst, we can threaten to tell Gene about you and her being together and she'll have to change her story or risk getting fired along with us."

"Jana is one thing," Vivian said. "I can deal with her. It's a lot harder to convince Gene that his son is stealing when he so obviously buys Nick's story."

"Don't worry. I rigged the budget."

Vivian stopped pacing. "You got our money back?"

"Nope. I gave Boston even more money. Now Nick is taking the same amount of money he takes from us from all of Gio's branches. Including New York. Gene might trust Nick when it's him versus us, but when the entire company starts complaining about the same problem and NY's own money is being siphoned from him, he's not going to be able to ignore the issue. It won't be long before Gene's phone will be ringing off the hook."

With that, Vivian's own phone went off. The whimsical ringtone that filled the air felt fitting, like the soundtrack to the party they'd be throwing once Nick's nefarious deeds finally came to a screeching halt.

"It's a text from Gene."

"What's it say?"

"Change in plans. We're meeting him in his office upstairs."

"What did I tell you?"

Rose was the first one to stand and test the door. Part of her felt like a prisoner escaping jail, but she knew she was innocent. She was more than ready for her trial. The elevator ride up to the top floor stretched on forever, but Rose didn't mind. She liked the feeling of being on top.

Gene's office was swanky. There was no other way to say it. Where Vivian's office was as drab as the rest of the DC office, Gene's personal space was highly decorated with awards on shelves and plaques on the walls and designer furniture and a desk bigger than anything Rose had seen before. It was a bit too extravagant, but Rose would be lying if she said she wouldn't go over the top if she was the CEO of a major company and were rich enough to blow that kind of cash. The place was nice, and even if they were in trouble, Rose couldn't help but feel luxurious as she sank into one of the chairs before Gene's desk.

Nick stood in the corner of the room like a statue. His eyes followed Rose and Vivian as they took their seats, and Rose could feel his glare on the side of her face as she settled.

With everyone present, Gene cut right to the chase.

"After a quick check, it seems that someone did indeed alter the pay schedule." Gene looked pointedly at Rose. "Now, I can't point fingers without doing my research, but you can be sure that there will be a full-scale investigation, both for today's problem and the one Vivian is reporting in DC. If there have been any issues with funding at any time over the last few years, my team is going to find them. You can be sure that I'll get to the bottom of this, and you can be sure that everyone is going to get the pay they deserve."

Gene's speech was like music to Rose's ears. This was exactly what she wanted.

When she glanced to the corner, Nick's face was paler than usual. Even his scar was an eerie shade of silver. Normally, the sight of Nick did nothing but repulse her, but man, was it good to see him sweat. The only better sight was the smile on Vivian's lips.

Chapter 12

BACK IN THE HOTEL ROOM, Vivian had done little but wait for Gene to call. She sat at the desk for hours at a time, periodically checking her messages and pretending to watch the reality show Rose had tuned in to on the television. It was a miserable, lazy existence, but there was little more they could do than wait. Vivian wasn't her normal talkative self, and Rose was surprised when she broke her silence at midday.

"Rose?" she asked tentatively. "Can you get something out of my suitcase for me?"

Rose was out of her seat in no time, ready to serve in any way she could. "Sure, what do you need?"

"I believe it's on the bottom," Vivian said. "You'll know it when you see it."

That was ominous enough to give Rose some pause. She suddenly remembered how nervous Vivian had been when dealing with airport security, like she knew she was doing something wrong and was afraid of getting caught. She hadn't smuggled a weapon onto the plane, had she? Surely Rose wasn't going to find a gun and a box of bullets with Nick's name on them buried at the bottom of Vivian's suitcase. That was one way to get rid of their problem, but it was a bit too drastic, even for Rose.

Vivian's suitcase was packed as if an engineer had designed each and every piece of clothing to fit together perfectly within it.

Everything from her socks to her scarf were organized and packed tight, and there was a clear divide between Vivian's half of the suitcase and Jana's. Rose avoided the latter half, not caring to see what other pairs of underwear Jana had left at Vivian's apartment. She assumed whatever Vivian was looking for was on her own side anyway. Carefully, she removed the clothing, leaving them folded the way they were in the case as she set them on the bedspread and slowly dug her way toward the bottom.

Rose didn't know what she expected to uncover, but this wasn't it.

Vivian had brought the dildo.

She quickly spun around to question Vivian about why she had this with her, only to find Vivian staring back at her with the answer already on her tongue.

"I was going to give it back to you. I can't keep it at the office, and I certainly wasn't going to bring it home with me. I thought maybe you would be able to return it and get your money back. Now, however…if you'd like to use it, we can."

Rose didn't even have to think about it.

"Please tell me you have scissors so I can open this thing."

"Of course I do, I'm a lesbian," Vivian said, sounding mildly offended. "They're in my bathroom bag."

Rose raced to the bathroom like she needed the scissors to cut the fuse on a bomb instead of the plastic packaging wrapped around the dildo. She was just as quick to free it, and for the first time Rose could actually test what the toy felt like. It was squishy, but firm. Its silicone gave way to her touch, but retained enough of its rigidity that she could easily use it to pleasure herself. Or Vivian.

After marveling for a moment at the cool feel of the bright red cylinder in her palm, she carried it out of the restroom for Vivian to observe, waving it high on the air like an Olympic torch. Vivian laughed again, because seriously, how could anyone not? It was a giant, red dick for Christ's sake. But she stared at the phallus in wonder, too, like she was excited for what it could entail.

Rose was right there with her.

"Have you ever used one before?" Rose asked.

Vivian nodded. "Yes. With my ex. And Jana. I didn't bring my harness with me, though. I didn't assume I would need it."

"Me either."

"You've used them before, too, I take it?"

"I've been with girls who had them, but I don't actually own any myself. Well," she said. "Except this one. I bought two of these when I got them, but I haven't used mine yet."

"Do you want to use it now?" Vivian asked. Rose could sense the anticipation laced on her tongue.

"Do you mean now now or now later?" Rose asked.

Vivian shrugged. "Now whenever you want."

"I thought you were supposed to be waiting for Gene to call," Rose said. "You don't have time to be shoving a dildo inside of me."

Vivian blushed furiously, even more so than she normally did when the conversation turned to sex, and even though Vivian claimed she'd done this before, something told Rose it was still fairly novel.

"Does it weird you out that it's shaped like an actual penis?" Rose asked. "I know you've used strap-ons before, but you can get dildos that don't look exactly like male genitalia. I can't imagine this is a lesbian's first choice."

"It doesn't bother me much," Vivian said, scrutinizing the life-like mold in Rose's hand. "It's not like it's the real thing. And it can't be that reminiscent of it. I may not have seen many naked men in my time, but I don't think their genitals are supposed to be bright red unless they have some kind of STI."

Rose laughed. The dildo *did* kind of look like it might be diseased. She observed the phallus in a new light now, looking it over once more and rolling it between her palms in a gesture that looked much more like she was trying to give a hand job than she intended. Catching Vivian staring so intently at her movements was merely coincidental.

"Does it weird you out that I've been with men before?" Rose asked. "I can't tell if you're turned on or freaked out right now. I'm hoping it's the former."

132

"The thought of you in any sexual situation is…appealing," Vivian said. "I don't care who you've slept with before me. Or how you got off. You're hot. You're even hotter when you're having sex."

That was a compliment Rose would take any day.

"Good. Now would you like to see me in another sexual situation or would you like to sit at your desk a bit longer and wait for the phone to ring?" Rose leaned forward in her chair, very aware of how visible her cleavage was and how Vivian's eyes tracked the low cut of her shirt. She was also very aware of how biased she was toward one particular answer to that question.

Vivian almost looked like she might cave until she managed a begrudging groan. "Don't remind me about work. I'm dreading this meeting. I know it's likely to go in our favor, but I'm still worried."

"Sounds like you need a break," Rose said, tapping the head of the dildo against her chin thoughtfully. Vivian looked at her like she knew all too well what that smirk on Rose's face meant.

"Are you implying what I think you are?"

"Are you thinking that I should fuck you with this dildo right now?"

Vivian still looked hesitant, but she wasn't saying no. Rose figured they'd better do this the right way.

"What's your safeword?" she asked.

"Safeword."

"Yeah, safeword. You know that thing you shout when someone is doing something you'd rather they not be doing?"

"No, I mean my safeword is *safeword*," Vivian said.

Rose rolled her eyes. "That's the most boring, unoriginal safeword I've ever heard in my life. Why am I not surprised?"

"What's yours?" Vivian asked.

"Atherosclerosis," Rose said effortlessly.

Vivian was quiet for a moment. "Well, you're right, that did give me pause. Nothing says 'turn off' quite like heart disease."

Rose hummed in agreement. "Sex is a good way to combat it, though." She winked.

"I don't trust myself to say atherosclerosis properly," Vivian disclosed, mouth struggling to form the word even then. "If I just say stop will you stop?"

"Of course."

"Then I guess you can fuck me," she said, most of the reluctance gone from her voice.

Rose smiled happily. "Good. While we're talking about it, are there any other things you wouldn't be comfortable with that I should know about?"

"I wouldn't want to watch you sleep with someone else," Vivian said firmly. "I'm not into the whole sharing thing."

"No threesomes?" Rose asked sadly. "You don't want to call up Jana and have both of us on you at once? She could bring the harness." Rose was teasing, making herself come across as much more willing to go through with this plan than she actually was. Would she ever have a threesome with Vivian? Maybe. Would she ever have a threesome with Jana? When hell froze over.

"I don't know if you and Jana would get along," Vivian said. Somehow Rose already knew that. "You're too similar. I think you'd both just be fighting for control the whole time."

"So we could have hot hate sex," Rose said.

"Still not my thing."

"Duly noted." Rose was fine with that. More than fine with that. Jana wasn't exactly someone she found herself fantasizing about.

Vivian, however, she wanted to get her hands on. Always.

Sex talk out of the way, she moved on to the real thing, sliding her hand along the back of Vivian's neck and pulling her in for a kiss that was as breathtaking as discovering that dildo in Vivian's suitcase. The kiss lasted until nothing else was on their mind, until Vivian's work was completely forgotten. If she didn't need oxygen almost as much as she needed Vivian, Rose never would have pulled away. There were benefits that came with ending a good kiss, though.

"How about we take this to the bed?"

The most Vivian could muster was a nod as Rose rose to her feet.

She took Vivian's hand, helping her off the chair and guiding her the few feet over to the bed. Vivian shed the rest of her clothes on the way there, tossing her shirt and bra neatly over the back of the desk chair along with her pants, but leaving her underwear on for Rose to take off herself.

As soon as she was near naked, Vivian set off to even the playing field, undressing Rose with expert speed that came from days of doing this now, tearing off Rose's clothes to reveal the supple bulge of her breasts and the perfect skin of her thighs. Rose liked the way Vivian gaped at her, eyes wide and mesmerized as she undressed her, and Rose rewarded her by slipping a hand down the front of her dampened underwear as they stood beside the bed.

"You're so wet for me," Rose said, diving her fingers into the pool between Vivian's thighs and letting them swim among the juices for a moment as Vivian bit her lip and tried not to moan. "I guess I shouldn't be surprised," Rose said. "It takes a lot to ruin a pair of underwear. I hope you've packed a couple of spares. It'd be a shame if you had to go commando."

Running drenched fingers over Vivian's clit and spreading her cum across the length of Vivian's sex probably wasn't helping the soaked panties situation, but Rose didn't care. She needed Vivian as wet as possible, wanted to see the evidence of her arousal staining the front of the thin, black material around her hips to know that she was ready for what was to come.

With a bit more rubbing, Rose could not only see Vivian's arousal but smell it, too, and the heady scent of Vivian filled the air as Rose dropped to her knees again, sliding the soaked material down Vivian's thighs with her.

"Lay on the bed," Rose said, standing again and twirling Vivian's underwear around her index finger. The smell was even more potent up close, and Rose was forced to drape the underwear across the back of the wooden desk chair with the rest of Vivian's clothes before she became too tempted to stick her face in, getting a whiff of Vivian straight from the source.

Vivian killed no time in lying flat against the mattress, cool sheets conforming to the slope of her spine and the curve of her ass as she waited for Rose to join her and give another command.

Rose retrieved the dildo and climbed atop Vivian and the mattress, hovering the weight of her body over Vivian's as she leaned down to kiss her, tongue scraping her bottom lip and prying entrance into Vivian's mouth. They kissed for a moment, heavy and opened-mouthed, until Vivian wrapped a leg around Rose's waist and Rose's arms started to give out beneath her. Vivian whined in protest at the separation of their lips, but Rose made up for it by biting at Vivian's bottom lip and whispering into the flesh, "Do you want me inside of you, Vivian?"

"Yes," Vivian said, and Rose kissed her again in reward.

"Spread your legs for me."

Vivian obeyed, rotating her hips outward and exposing her sex to the air as Rose lay down beside her, placing the dildo against her lips where she sucked the head into her mouth to wet it. If she had known this was going to happen, she would have bought Vivian a bottle of lube as her second Christmas present instead of soaps, but she hadn't and spit would have to do for now.

"If I go too fast tell me to slow down," Rose said. Vivian nodded her head in approval.

Carefully, Rose positioned the head of the dildo near Vivian's entrance, twirling the phallus and coating the circumference of the tip in Vivian's juices before running it down the length of Vivian's slit, the underside of the head scraping against Vivian's twitching clit.

"Please." Vivian was begging, and Rose figured there was no possible way Vivian could ever be wetter than she was right now.

She lowered the dildo toward Vivian's center again, this time pushing slowly forward and watching the head disappear inside of Vivian's walls. Vivian groaned from the pressure and Rose looked up again, making sure she was okay.

"Feel good?" she asked, voice sultry, but compassionate.

Vivian nodded, lips wrapped around her teeth in a harsh bite. "So good. More."

Green-lighted, Rose pushed forward again, helping Vivian's walls absorb more of the shaft. The insertion was easier this time around. The head was the bulkier portion of the toy, and Vivian was starting to adjust to the foreign feeling of the dildo inside her. With how wet Vivian was, the silicone slid in easily, almost all the way to the base before it was met with resistance. Rose didn't force it. She pulled it back out partway, only to gently shove it back inside, the veins of the dildo rubbing against the ridges of Vivian's walls.

Vivian's eyes were closed in pleasure at this point, head thrown back onto the pillow as she surrendered herself to Rose, letting the woman on top of her do whatever she pleased.

"You're so tight," Rose said, paying close attention to the miniscule movements of her wrist but looking back to Vivian every once in a while to gauge Vivian's reaction or leave a kiss against the side of her neck or her cheek for reassurance. "You're so wet, too. Hear that?" Beneath the harshness of Vivian's breathing and the pounding of her heart in her ears, Rose could hear the wet slap of Vivian's flesh, the noise intensifying the faster Rose moved.

Subconsciously, Vivian's legs opened wider, allowing even easier access that Rose was quick to take advantage of, testing Vivian's boundaries and pressing the dildo into her down to its base, until only Rose's fingers at the bottom of the toy prevented it from going all the way in.

Vivian was moaning again, louder than the sound of the toy driving inside of her, and every time Rose pumped in and out, hitting Vivian's G-spot on each stroke, the whimpers only increased in volume. Rose almost considered muffling the sounds with a pillow, but she didn't want to cover up the sight of Vivian's face scrunched deliciously in pleasure as she neared her edge. She wanted to watch Vivian cum, and when her face started to unravel, Rose coaxed her on, giving one final, solid push on the dildo and whispering to Vivian, "Cum for me."

The force of Vivian's orgasm nearly pushed the dildo out of her on its own, but Rose held it firmly in place, allowing Vivian to ride out her orgasm against the thick of it, her walls stretched around the silicone as they spasmed. Vivian thanked her with another string of moans, and Rose didn't pull out until Vivian was still against her side, body tense as Rose exited her even more slowly than she had entered. Her body released the dildo with a pop and she let out a solid groan, one not quite as gratifying for Rose to hear.

"I'm going to be so sore tomorrow," Vivian said, turning her head to smile at Rose. "So worth it, though."

"I hope you're not too tired yet, because it's my turn."

Rose handed Vivian the dildo to free her hands to take off her own ruined underwear and straddle Vivian, sitting completely naked atop Vivian's hips.

Vivian looked distracted by the sight in front of her. She was riveted by Rose's breasts, and Rose was forced to tear Vivian's gaze away.

"If you don't fuck me now, I'll have no problem taking that dildo off your hands and using it on myself."

The threat knocked Vivian back into reality, and she speedily positioned the dildo between Rose and herself, letting Rose do most of the work as she sunk down onto the cock, taking the tip and most of the shaft with ease. Vivian marveled at how easily the dildo slipped inside her.

"Fuck, you must be soaked."

"Watching a hot girl orgasm at your hand will do that to you," Rose said, bouncing gently on the dick held steady by Vivian's hand. "It helps that you already came all over it. Your cum works better than lube."

Rose's heart rate picked up at the feeling of the dildo completely inside her, covered in Vivian's juices. She hadn't been fucked this thoroughly in months and she couldn't help it that her movements turned frantic, grinding against the dildo for any friction she could get. She couldn't remember the last time sex felt this good. (Yes she could. Sex was always this good with Vivian. Every time seemed to feel better than the last.)

Still, she cursed herself for not using this dildo sooner. To think she had this experience available at home all along and had never taken advantage of it. She'd have to thank Phoebe sometime for recommending this to her. After this week, she was going to be back to spending a lot of time pleasuring herself and it was nice to know that she had at least something to look forward to in the sex department back in DC.

Vivian was speechless as she helped Rose fuck herself, thrusting the dildo up in time with the sink of Rose's hips and using her free hand to explore Rose's chest, cupping each breast as it bounced in her palm. Rose cursed each time Vivian's thumb grazed a nipple or the dildo hit a particularly sensitive spot inside of her, and it wasn't long before it was getting more and more difficult for her to maintain her cool.

"This feels so good, Vivian." She moaned. "I might come even faster than you did in the shower the other day."

Vivian's hand stalled its motions at the insult. Rose whined her dissent. "Please don't stop."

Vivian could never be so cruel. She picked up her movements again, increasing her speed twofold, and soon Rose's gratefulness was lost in a sea of expletives and repetitions of Vivian's name. Before long, she was coming faster and harder than Vivian, and Vivian had to sit up against the headboard to hold Rose close as her body wracked with spasms.

When Rose opened her eyes again, Vivian was staring back at her like she was the greatest sight in New York. Rose bumped their foreheads together, keeping their faces close as they kissed lazily between smiles and Vivian extricated the dildo out of Rose and out from beneath the sheets. Rose could stay this way forever, poised in Vivian's lap with their lips permanently attached. Vivian looked like maybe she could, too. Although she looked more contemplative than Rose, clearly letting her mind race while Rose tried to slow hers down and absorb the moment while it lasted.

Chapter 13

ROSE WAS STARTING TO GET acquainted with Gene's office. She liked that.

"We're going to headquarters again?" she asked.

Vivian nodded. "Gene called. He said the investigation's over and that we'd 'want to see the results.'" She made air quotes around the phrase and mimicked Gene's serious tone.

"Took him long enough."

"It hasn't even been a week."

"I could've done it in a day."

Vivian rolled her eyes. "We're not all as gifted as you."

"What time does he want us there?"

"Early this afternoon."

"Should we start packing early, then?"

The hotel room wasn't a mess, but it wasn't clean either. It had that lived-in feeling. There were dirty clothes on the desk, empty water bottles on the night stands, a full trash can in the kitchen. They had only been staying in the room for a week, but cleaning was the last thing on either of their minds when they were in it.

"You make it sound like we're getting fired," Vivian said. "Don't be so morose. It's Nick who should be afraid for his job."

Rose knew that. She wasn't scared about the meeting. She was scared about leaving. The past week had been eventful, to say the least. She liked this new routine of spending all her time with Vivian and exploring a totally new environment. Combine that with the thrill of overthrowing a corrupt corporate power structure, and she didn't know if she'd be able to readjust to normal life back home.

"We can start packing when we get back," she said.

"Good idea. I'm too nervous to clean."

Vivian was jittery throughout the cab ride to headquarters. She fiddled constantly with her outfit or stared into the cab driver's mirror to adjust her hair. It made Rose antsy just to watch. Halfway through the ride, she reached over and took Vivian's hand in her own. It was a stark contrast to what they'd done in the back of a cab the night they'd left the bar, but Rose liked this, too. Her own composure felt grounded as she tried to ground Vivian's. They held hands all the way to headquarters' front doors, and Rose missed it as they separated and rode the elevator up to Gene.

Gene's office was exactly as Rose remembered it. Not a strand of carpet fiber was out of place, and even Nick was in the same corner as before, looking just as devastated as he had at the end of the last meeting. Rose sank into the seat in front of Gene's desk with comfortable familiarity. Just seeing Nick pout put her in a good mood.

"I won't beat around the bush," Gene said. "We all know why we're here." He lifted a few papers from his desk, then set them back down again. "Thanks to this little stunt, I had my team methodically examine exactly what happened. Vivian, the funds were altered from your account, but, as you were in the room with me when the alteration occurred, I can only assume that Rose will take credit for the job?"

Gene's calculated coolness didn't sound promising for Rose's future, but she wasn't about to ruin Vivian's without warrant. "Yes, sir."

"But aside from that, we also found that DC has been missing a considerable amount of funds for quite some time." His eyes shifted to Nick. "And that Boston has been receiving an excess of funds for quite some time, ironically the same amount of time that DC has been losing them." Gene's tone was no longer that of a calm professional, but of a disappointed father.

Nick dropped his head and stared down at the floor.

Gene wasn't having that. "Nick?" he asked, forcing his son to look up and face him again. "I believe you have something to say to Ms. Tracey?"

Nick bobbed on the toes of his dress shoes, glanced directly at Rose, then looked at some point on the wall just beyond her. He took a deep breath, then let out an unintelligible grumble. If Rose didn't know better, she'd almost think he'd apologized.

Gene cleared his throat, and Nick raised his voice reluctantly. "Sorry, okay?"

Gene was making his son apologize like a schoolboy who'd pulled Vivian's braids on the playground. It was the most pathetic thing Rose had ever seen in her life, and she was living for it.

"Thank you," Gene said. "You may leave now."

Nick's version of leaving was storming away and slamming the door behind him. Talk about temper tantrum. No wonder Gene was treating him like he was six.

The slam echoed in the silence, but Gene cleared his throat again and the awkwardness passed. The mood in the room improved considerably with Nick gone. "Sorry about that. And about what's been happening to you. I know sorry doesn't cover it, but I can assure you that from this point on DC is not going to be having any more financial troubles. I'll be personally reissuing you all the money you've been cheated out of, and I can promise that DC will soon be in better shape than it ever has been."

This was perfect. Rose couldn't have dreamed of a better outcome.

"What about Boston?" Vivian asked. "I hate to say this, Gene, but Nick is a terrible leader. Now that the Boston staff doesn't have the extra money to put them ahead, I'm afraid they're really going to suffer from this."

"Don't worry about Boston," Gene said. "And don't worry about my feelings either. I know my son has his issues." Gene's words were calm, but his eyes reflected a blueness that had more to do with his mood than his genes. "Which is why Nick has been removed from his position."

"You fired him?" Rose asked.

"Not quite. He's still useful to me. His methodology may be skewed, but his drive is something a father can be proud of. He's the new head of the Guatemala branch. If he's so desperate for money, maybe he can improve the South American offices for the better in his quest for it."

The petty part of Rose was upset Nick wasn't totally fired, but an even pettier part of her was glad he would be stuck trying to manage as poorly funded an office as Vivian had been forced to for the last few years. It wasn't a discharge from the hospital, but it was a taste of his own medicine, and Rose could live with that, especially if Nick couldn't. She had a feeling he would be kicking and screaming all the way down south. She also had a feeling he wouldn't be able to afford a first class flight.

Rose could tell that nothing was bittersweet for Vivian. She was beaming. "I think that's a wise decision, sir."

Gene was modestly proud. "There are still a few tricks up these old sleeves. Not as clever as yours, though, Rose."

Rose wasn't clever. Just smart. "It was nothing."

"No, I'm being serious. I don't necessarily approve of how you did it, but I'm very impressed with what you managed to do. You're a lot more useful than your data entry position gave you credit for. Vivian was smart to see that in you."

Vivian looked at Rose. Her smile was a mix of pride in the both of them. Rose smiled back more joyously. It made her happier to see Vivian happy.

"Thank you, sir."

"You say you're still in school?"

Rose nodded.

"Well, when you graduate, you've got a full-time job here. Doing something much more suited to your skills than data entry. I can assure you that."

That didn't sound so bad. Rose was looking forward to going back to school, but part of her would miss Gio, or at least miss Vivian and Phoebe, and if Vivian followed through on her promise, Rose might have some fun working with her mom, too.

She also wouldn't mind a raise.

"Now, there's still the issue of your relationship." Instantly, the smile was wiped from Rose's face. "I need you to be honest with me. Are you romantically involved?"

Vivian looked to Rose. Rose looked back. There was no point in lying.

"Yes."

Gene nodded. "I appreciate the honesty. Well, as you know, office relationships are forbidden, and I can't let this continue the way it is."

Rose stared solemnly into her lap. At first it had seemed humorous to her that the DC branch was full of office relationships. Phoebe and Harley. Bailey and Mason. They got a laugh out of the forbidden nature of their affairs, but sitting here with Gene now, she and Vivian didn't feel like a joke. She should have expected this. Vivian was off limits, and she'd have to pay the price for crossing that boundary at some point. Maybe she wouldn't lose her job for it, but losing Vivian sounded almost as bad, even if it was a noble sacrifice.

Gene surprised her by offering a much better alternative.

"So I'm implementing a new policy. As long as you document the relationship with HR and we have it on record so there's complete transparency, I have no issue with it."

"Really?" Rose asked.

Gene nodded. "As far as I see it, the alternative would be firing you, and you're both too valuable for me to do that. I want you around as long as you're willing to stay. If that means changing a small policy to accommodate you, it's the least I can do."

Rose was ecstatic. Her fingertips buzzed with the giddiness.

Vivian didn't sound quite as instantly relieved. "Both of us?" she asked. "It was Rose who did all the technical stuff. I just gave her the access."

"Yes, both of you. I'm impressed with you, too, Vivian. Even I would have had a hard time keeping DC afloat with the money problems you were having, and I certainly couldn't have done it when I was your age. You've got a great business head on your shoulders."

"She does," Rose said. "She's the one who knew there was a problem. I just found out what the problem was."

Gene smiled. "You make a good team, then."

Vivian smiled at Rose. "We do."

"I hope this little excursion hasn't completely ruined your trip," Gene said. "I know this wasn't exactly a vacation."

"Are you kidding?" Rose asked. In the last week she had visited New York for the first time, slept with her boss, saved her office from the schemes of a corrupt businessman, and gotten a full-time job offer lined up for after graduation. "This was the best week we could have hoped for."

Rose's words put a genuine smile on Gene's face. Rose was glad to make him happy. He was a good man, even if he hadn't fathered one.

"I'm glad to hear it. I think that's enough for the day. And the week. And the rest of the quarter. You're free to go, but I hope you both get a chance to come back to New York soon."

More than likely, Rose wouldn't get a chance to accompany Vivian on a business trip again, but she'd love to come back sometime, even if only on a personal vacation. Maybe she could afford one someday. There was still so much she hadn't seen. "I'd love to."

Vivian was the first to stand. When she stretched out her arm to Gene, he shook her hand genially. "Thank you, Gene. You've helped us out a lot."

"I think you two have helped me even more."

It was a good feeling leaving the office. Rose was proud of what they had done.

The first thing Vivian did when they got to the elevator was give Rose a celebratory victory kiss.

"Ready to pack?" she asked.

"Ready as I'll ever be."

Chapter 14

Waking up would have been easier if Vivian didn't still have to pack.

They'd wasted away the night before in bed, and as a result it was crunch time. Vivian was up and at 'em even earlier than Rose had gotten up for the airport on the day she'd left for this trip. Watching Vivian stuff her suitcase to the breaking point was not that entertaining. If they'd have done this last night, as Rose had suggested, then they would have had time to have sex this morning before they left.

But then again, if Vivian had packed last night, they wouldn't have had time to have sex then either.

There was no winning this battle.

"If you get up now, we can hit the continental breakfast before we have to go to the airport," Vivian tried to tempt her.

Breakfast did sound good. Rose remembered eating a lot last night, but most of that was Vivian's pussy and very little of it was actual food. "I'm hungry, but I don't want to move," she groaned.

"Want me to go get you something?" Vivian asked. "I think they let you bring stuff up to the rooms."

"Could you?" Rose said, gratefully. "You don't have to if it won't leave you with enough time to finish packing."

"I have time," Vivian said. "You helped me get some of my stuff together yesterday, remember? The least I can do is go get you food. Give and take, right?"

"Yeah," Rose said, relaxing into the bed sheets and relishing the cool feel of them against her skin. "Thank you."

Rose was on the brink of drifting off to sleep again, body wedged into the patch of warmth Vivian had imprinted on the sheets during the night, when Vivian returned, coffee, bagels, and donuts in hand. The baked goods rested on a thick pile of napkins already coated in sprinkles of cracked glazing. Greedily, Rose snatched a few rings from Vivian, not caring how many crumbs fell onto the sheets. She was never going to sleep here again, after all.

Rose enjoyed her breakfast as she watched Vivian pack between taking sips of coffee and bites of her bagel. She worked meticulously, but at a good pace, and she was on to packing her bathroom stuff before Rose even thought about getting up and taking a shower.

She wasn't going to, she decided. She could shower when she got home. Plus, she kind of liked having the scent of Vivian on her from the night before. The musk of her sweat was evidence of the way their bodies had been joined. Not knowing when or if she would ever smell that way again, she wasn't ready to give up the feeling yet.

Coffee in her veins, Rose got up, put on her last clean outfit, and went to the bathroom to put her makeup on and gather her things while Vivian did the same.

The bedroom felt empty when it was so clean. Vivian's laptop was no longer on the desk, no clothes littered the floor, what little food had been left on the kitchen counter was stuffed away into their bags, and apart from the rumpled sheets and full trash can, no one would guess that two girls had been living here for the past week. It didn't look the same as it did while inhabited, and Rose didn't feel as sad about leaving it behind as she thought she would.

Her luggage felt heavier than it did when she'd first carried it upstairs, though. Probably because she had stashed a giant, mostly uneaten bag of animal crackers in one of the side pockets of her suitcase near the dildo. She hadn't had time to put either of them inside of her as much as she would have liked during this trip, and she planned to make up for that lost time as soon as she got home.

The clerk at the front desk was the same one who had greeted them their first day here, some boy fresh out of high school who barely knew what he was doing as he took their key cards and checked them out of the system.

"Did you have a nice time?" he asked them, trying to distract from his incompetence with small talk. Rose was more distracted by the huge zit on the end of his nose.

"Yes, thank you," Vivian said. She forced a polite smile upon her face.

"New York is great for romantic getaways," he said as he punched some keys on the computer.

This kid looked like he had never talked to a girl in his life. Rose couldn't tell if it was his inexperience with dating that made him assume she and Vivian were a couple or his vast experience with jacking off to lesbian porn that made him project his fantasies onto the two of them.

She refused to think that it may have been because they were acting like a couple.

Put off as she was, she was still going to play along and have fun with him.

"Yes, it is," she agreed, reaching out and threading her arm through Vivian's. Vivian seemed surprised at first, but caught on to the game and swayed gently closer to Rose's side.

"Do you ladies want me to call a cab for you?" the boy asked, clearly overeager for the opportunity. Rose wanted to treat him like a dog and tell him to calm down.

"We're good," Vivian said. "We can get one ourselves."

"Oh." He pouted, then handed Vivian the final papers. "Well, you're all checked out now. I hope you enjoyed your stay."

The exchange was awkward, but on the boy's part more than anyone's, and as soon as Rose and Vivian were out the hotel doors, they were laughing about it, joking about their "romantic getaway" all the way to the airport gate. It was only when they found themselves on the plane in their seats that their conversation died down. Rose's voice felt hoarse from talking so much, but if this was going to be her last morning with Vivian, she was going to milk it.

And speaking of milking things, there was no reason they shouldn't try to get the most of this plane flight.

"Excuse me." Rose flagged down a flight attendant whose name tag read "Jake." He was skinny and young, near Rose's age, but definitely a couple years younger. He stopped for Rose like her word was law. He was new, if Rose had to guess, and scared of not doing his job satisfactorily. "Do you know if there's a stewardess named Heather on this flight or is this not her shift?"

"I'm afraid not, ma'am," he said. "Heather was recently fired."

Rose gave Vivian a scandalized look before turning back to Jake. "Why?"

His eyes shifted uncomfortably. "That's information I'm not allowed to reveal to passengers."

That just made Rose want to find out even more. She lowered her voice to a whisper for Jake's sake, signaling to him that she didn't want his superiors to overhear the conversation either. "No, but, really. What does a flight attendant get fired for anyway? Giving someone the wrong bag of peanuts?"

"More like having sex with passengers in the bathroom."

Jake walked away, and Rose turned back to Vivian who looked like she was enjoying this gossip almost as much as Rose. "So much for seducing her into first class again," Rose said. "I guess we'll have to live with coach."

"You could flirt with Jake and get him to do it. He's probably into older women."

"One, how dare you call me old, and two, I'm not in the mood to flirt today."

"You've been flirting with me all morning," Vivian said. "Or did you forget about the romantic getaway we're supposedly on?"

"Ok, I'm not in the mood to flirt with anyone other than you."

"I'm strangely okay with that."

"Good."

Coach was...less than pleasant and definitely not up to Rose's standards if she spent too much time looking around, but for the majority of the flight she barely cared.

She had the occasional reminder, like when the woman in front of her reclined her seat until it was about four inches away from her face. Or the way her legs cramped when she was unable to stretch them out for fear of kicking the seat of the woman in front of her, although she indulged once or twice. Vivian was a good enough distraction. They could easily talk their way through the next hour, though Rose did try to keep their conversation hushed for the sake of any eavesdropping passengers. Most people around them were either asleep, in the middle of their own conversations, or listening to the in-flight movie on their headphones, but she could never be too careful.

"This is going to be a long flight," Vivian noted, eyeing the chair practically in Rose's face, sympathetic but also glad the woman's husband in front of her wasn't quite as rude as his wife.

"You wanna sneak off to the bathroom and join the mile-high club? That'll kill some time."

"As much as I would love to have sex with you, I don't want to do it in an airplane bathroom."

"Does that mean our vacation sex spree is officially over?" Rose asked. "Unless you want to have sex with me in the airport bathroom, I think we're running out of opportunities."

"The airport restroom is probably even less sanitary," Vivian said. "I think we are officially done having sex on this vacation." She was quiet for a moment before she added, "There's still plenty of time after vacation, though. Gene more or less gave us his consent."

"Secret hookups with your employee." Rose tried to hide her excitement. "That's hot. I like it."

Vivian face blushed hot as Rose egged her on, but she spoke coolly and calmly with a shrug of her shoulders. "It doesn't always have to be about sex. We could just hang out, too. Get drinks sometime."

"And then fuck in the back of a cab?"

"We can't have public sex in DC. Someone might recognize me, and I can't live with that embarrassment for the rest of my life."

"I guess what happens in New York stays in New York, huh?"

"Not all of it. Just that part. We can still do drinks. And find places to go together. Have you been to all the monuments in DC?"

"A lot of them. But not all of them," Rose said.

"Then maybe I can show you around the ones you haven't been to," Vivian said.

"Deal. Then we can get dinner together, too."

"I know a few good bars I haven't been barred from."

"Sightseeing, dinner, and drinks? Kinda sounds like you just agreed to take me out on a date."

"I didn't call it that," Vivian said. "But if that's what you think constitutes a date, we've been dating for an entire week now."

"Maybe I'm okay with that," Rose said.

"Maybe I am too."

Rose's heart was racing. She and Vivian were sort of joking around. They hadn't actually made serious plans to start dating. There were no official titles, no grand declarations of romance, just a promise of maybe, and that was enough for Rose. "Maybe" left her with enough time to sort out her feelings, to know if she just missed being in a relationship or if it was Vivian she really wanted. It would also give her time to figure out if she wanted to keep in touch with Vivian outside of work when she went back to college in a few weeks.

Plus, she was having too much fun to complicate things just yet. There was no sense in ruining something good, and what she and Vivian had was great.

When she stepped off the plane, Rose wasn't as sad for the vacation to be over as she had expected to be. As much as she had been dreading coming home, boy did it suddenly feel nice to be back in DC. She could go home, see her mom, sleep in her own bed, *do laundry*. She was still sad to part ways with Vivian for the first time in six days, but she would trade the separation anxiety for a home-cooked meal.

Rose stood at the gate with her luggage in hand, swaying awkwardly beside Vivian who stretched her lengthy limbs like she'd been cooped up in the plane for several hours instead of slightly more than one.

This was the part where they said their good-byes, where Rose would be forced to discover the magic words that would leave Vivian missing her and wanting more. She had nothing, though. There was nothing profound or clever to say, just a desperate desire to make small talk and stall until they reached the parking lot and maybe even past that. Maybe by some miracle Vivian's apartment was only a few blocks from Rose's house and they could take a final cab ride together. Maybe Rose could see where Vivian lived.

That plan changed when they spotted Jana waiting for them by the baggage claim.

Rose was secretly hoping her mom or Phoebe might greet her at the airport, but Jana was the last person she expected to be here and the last person she wanted to see. A sense of dread and rage washed over her all at once, and it instantly ruined Rose's good mood.

Vivian stiffened at the sight of her. If the look on her face was any indication, she was ready to hop on the baggage carousel and let it whisk her away.

"I got your luggage," Jana said, holding up Vivian's suitcase. "I remembered what it looked like."

Rose's bag was mysteriously not present by Jana's side. Rose saw it whirl past and moved away to try and grab it, but kept close enough to eavesdrop.

"What are you doing here?" Vivian asked.

"I just came to say sorry," Jana said.

"For what? Almost getting me fired? Helping Nick get away with embezzlement when you knew I'd suspected him of scamming us for years?"

"I was mad," Jana said. "I know that's a bad excuse."

"You're right, it is."

"This is because of her, isn't it?"

Rose was obviously the "her" in question. She stood by the carousel and tried to blend in with the crowd as she looked for her luggage like all the other innocent passersby.

"It's about you putting the company in danger," Vivian said. "You should know better."

"I thought you knew better than to cheat on me."

"We weren't a couple."

"So you thought."

Rose's bag rounded the corner. She grabbed it. Crap. Now she had no excuse to stand next to the belt. She shot Vivian a panicked look and prayed to God she would look Rose's way. Her prayers were answered.

"We can't do this here," Vivian said to Jana. "If you take me home, we can talk this out on the way."

Jana nodded. She was so frazzled even her hair seemed to stand on end.

Vivian met Rose at the conveyer belt. "I'm sorry," she said, and Rose believed it. "I didn't think she'd come here."

"It's not your fault."

"Are you okay with getting a cab alone?"

Vivian had planned on taking a cab with her back to the city. Rose was too distracted by this to care that she'd have to travel alone now. "Yeah, of course."

"I promise I'll have this sorted out in the morning."

Rose looked back to Jana who fiddled with her hands anxiously as she waited. She was clearly an emotional wreck, and if Vivian couldn't sort everything out by morning, that was okay. Vivian was her fuck buddy, not her girlfriend. She didn't owe it to Rose to fix her entire messed up love life overnight.

"I'll see you at work tomorrow," Rose said, and she was genuinely looking forward to it.

Chapter 15

WHEN ROSE ENTERED THE HOUSE, she was greeted by the sweet tang of roasted chicken and simmering tomato sauce. After nothing but bar food and cheap groceries for an entire week, a hot, home-cooked meal was the best welcome home gift Rose's mom could give her, and Beth had delivered. From the smell alone, Rose knew exactly what the dish was—chicken parmesan, Rose's favorite.

The bang of pots rang out from the kitchen, and Rose's stomach lured her into the room. While her mother's back was turned, Rose couldn't resist sneaking up on her.

"Whatcha makin'?"

Startled, Beth fumbled with her pan, dropping it on the counter where it landed with an even louder clang than before, but her surprise gave way to excitement as she turned to see Rose standing behind her. "You're back!" Beth wrapped her in a hug. "I missed you, honey."

"I missed you, too, Mom."

"You have to tell me everything. How was your trip? Did everything go okay?"

Rose nodded. "Better than okay. Everything was great."

Their embrace was interrupted by the beeping of the stove. Beth hurried to check the food. "Set the table. I want you to tell me all about it."

Rose recounted the story while they ate. She told her mom about her first flight, about how beautiful New York had been even though she hadn't gotten a chance to see much of it, about how she and Vivian had worked together to weed out Nick and fix the budgeting issue across the branches.

The only thing she left out was the part about sleeping with her boss. It wasn't that she thought Beth would inherently disapprove, but there were no words to describe what she and Vivian were at the moment. There were no titles, no talks. Rose was close to her mother, but not close enough to disclose the details of her hookups. That was what Phoebe was for. Plus, Beth would be taking Rose's old job soon, once she left for school. Rose didn't want her mom's first impression of her new boss to be, *That's the woman who's sleeping with my daughter.*

"Gene even offered me a job after I finish school," Rose said as she wrapped up her story. "I don't know for sure if I'll take it yet. I'll definitely keep my options open, but it is nice to have some sense of job security in case nothing better comes along." Job security wasn't something Rose would have brought up a few weeks ago. Employment, or lack thereof, had been a sensitive subject, and Rose didn't want to make Beth feel guilty for losing her last position. Now, though, Beth didn't seem touchy about the conversation at all. She ate with carefree grace and smiled at Rose as she talked.

"That's great! I've got my own interview coming up, too, you know. I really can't thank you enough for putting in a good word for me, Rose."

It was hard to think that Rose had initially only agreed to this trip to help out her mom. Somewhere along the way it had become all about Vivian. And saving Gio Corp. from ultimate demise. But mostly Vivian. "It was no problem, Mom."

"I mean it." Beth's voice was softer. She was staring at Rose across the table with that mushy mom smile. "I'm really proud of you, Rose."

The compliment warmed her, and they ate the rest of their meal in contented silence. By the end of dinner, Rose caught herself yawning. She hadn't meant to crash so soon. She'd wanted to unpack a bit and call Phoebe, but that wasn't going to happen. She was tired, and the only thing she wanted to get reacquainted with was her bed. She'd see Phoebe tomorrow. She wanted to get to work early to greet Vivian anyway.

Rose jumped the gun by coming into work too early. She was so excited to see Vivian that she hadn't stopped to consider that Vivian didn't come into the office until nine.

Rose was still confined to Vivian's closet, but that didn't seem so bad now. She liked being close to Vivian, and she was going back to school in a couple of weeks. She could wait it out, at least until Vivian came and told her if she could have her old cubicle back. She set up shop at her glorified dinner tray and waited for Vivian.

When she heard Vivian enter, another voice came in with her.

"You want me to pack up my office, too?" The voice was unmistakably Jana's raspy whine.

"I don't think you should work here anymore." Vivian's voice was tired and defeated. How long had they been having this conversation?

Rose couldn't resist the temptation to stop what she was doing and listen.

"You have no right to fire me because you're mad at me."

"And you had no right to let Nick get away with fraud because you were mad at me." Vivian sighed. Her voice was calmer when she spoke again. "Besides, I'm not firing you. I suggested you should be transferred. Boston needs the extra help. Gene isn't exactly thrilled about you helping Nick, but I put in a good word for you, and he agreed that he can use you for the time being."

"You're just trying to push me out of the way."

"I'm trying to do what's best for both of us. You're better off in Boston with a raise and a clean slate. You're not going to do your best work here if you're distracted by what happened between us. Clearly, we're no longer capable of working together, and it's not like you want to stay here. It was your idea to spend all night packing up your things at my apartment."

Jana was quiet. They both were.

"Fine," Jana said. "I'll talk to Gene. And I'll drop your stuff off tonight." Footsteps shuffled about the carpet. The door creaked open. "Nice knowing you, Viv."

The slamming of the door that followed shook Rose. She sat there, quiet and still. It wasn't until she heard the squeak of Vivian plopping into her chair that she got the courage to move again.

Slowly, Rose stepped out of the closet.

Vivian's face looked as if a ghost had entered the room rather than one of her employees. "Rose!"

"Hey." She smiled lightly. "I heard what you said to Jana."

Vivian's sudden surprise gave way to her dejected state again. "Sorry. I didn't think you'd be here yet. I didn't mean to air out my dirty laundry in front of you like that."

Rose shrugged. "I lived with your dirty laundry for a week in New York."

Vivian blushed. Rose stepped closer and sat on the end of Vivian's desk.

"It was nice of you, what you did. Getting her that job in Boston."

"Not nice," Vivian said. "Just looking out for my employees."

"You didn't have to do that. Especially after what she did."

"Jana's a good person. Usually. If I stoop to her level, I'm no better than her."

"I know," Rose said. "I admire that about you."

"Yeah?"

"Yeah." Rose placed her hand over Vivian's. It was a subtle comfort, but it felt risqué in the office. Rose was all too aware of the windows surrounding them and the fact that they could be seen at any moment.

"Well, I have another meeting here soon," Vivian said. "It's an interview, so heads up if you want to skip out on that. I probably shouldn't be giving away personal information to employees hiding in the closet."

Rose jumped down from the desk.

"Sounds like the perfect time for a break." After eavesdropping on Vivian's and Jana's good-bye, she could use one.

Vivian laughed. "Work started less than an hour ago."

"Hey, I've been here longer than you," Rose said. "Plus, I can take my break whenever I want."

"Fine, but don't come crying to me when it's lunchtime and you have to eat over your computer because you're running behind."

That wouldn't be a first.

"I'll be back," Rose said, and she knew exactly where she was going.

Phoebe was right where Rose thought she'd be, her back turned away from the entrance of the cubicle and hard at work typing on…a new computer?

Rose didn't have time to question the updated technology. Phoebe's old monitor was sitting right next to the new one, dormant and unused, and the dark pane of glass acted like a mirror, giving away Rose's presence. Phoebe turned around and was up and out of the chair within seconds, arms around Rose in a hug harder than any Vivian had ever given her. The squeal she let out was loud enough to alarm half of the office, but Rose was too caught up in their reunion to care.

"You're back!"

"Yep." Rose smiled. "Just got here. Is that a new computer?"

"Yes! They came in this morning. Harley just finished setting mine up for me. It's awesome. I don't know what you and Vivian said to the owners while you were gone, but whatever you did, it worked. We're finally entering the twenty-first century!"

Talk about express delivery. Fuck Amazon Prime—Rose wanted whatever Gene used.

Phoebe wasn't the only one with a new computer. Rose's old desk held one, too. Her old side of the cubicle was still empty.

Rose sat down in her old chair and took a moment to let it all sink in. She'd hated most of her time in this cubicle, but now that she was leaving it, she felt nostalgic. She'd miss the quirks of working with Phoebe and the privacy of doing next to nothing all day and still getting paid for it because she never got caught.

"Are you ready for them to replace me?" Rose asked.

"It's bittersweet," Phoebe said. "I'll miss you, but I do like your mom."

"Just don't get mad at her because she can't measure up to me," Rose said.

"You're right. No one could ever measure up to the amount of time you wasted on the job. Your slacking was truly impressive."

"Thank you."

"Are you going to move back into the cubicle for your last few weeks, or does Vivian still have you tied up in her storage closet?"

"I think I want to stay there."

Phoebe raised an eyebrow.

"I'll be gone in a couple weeks anyway," Rose said. "It's not that big of deal."

"Uh-huh." Phoebe nodded knowingly. "Whatever you say."

Rose heard the footsteps before she saw who they belonged to, but it wasn't long before she watched Mason rush into their cubicle hand in hand with Bailey. Rose was more than happy to see them.

"Rose! You're back!" He abandoned his boyfriend's side to hug her, and she reciprocated the embrace, always glad to share the same space as Mason's positivity. Bailey was subtler with his affections, but he smiled at her warmly. Mason's good mood was rubbing off on him, too.

"For now," Rose said.

"We'll have to catch up later," Bailey said. "Vivian wants you in her office."

Rose pouted. She hadn't anticipated leaving her friends so soon. "Did she say why?"

"She just said she was expecting you."

Rose checked her watch. Her break wasn't over yet. She was confused, but curious. "The boss awaits," she said. "I'll check in with you guys later. It's so good to see everyone again."

"Call me tonight," Phoebe said. "We're hanging out soon."

"You got it."

When Rose walked back to Vivian's office, she expected to find Vivian waiting for her. She didn't expect to find anyone else.

"Mom? What are you doing here?"

It was then that Rose noticed her formal attire, darks slacks and a nice blazer. It was such a change from how she was used to seeing her mom over the last few months, camped out on the couch in old sweatpants.

"I had an interview," Beth said. "I think it went fairly well." She smiled at Vivian knowingly. Vivian smiled back.

"Very well. So well, you can start this week."

Rose was beyond ecstatic. She felt as good as her mother looked. There was just one problem. "Why are you giving my job away when I still have two weeks left?"

"Someone has to train Beth," Vivian said. "Plus, we don't need you for data entry anymore. You're my personal assistant." Vivian winked from behind Beth. Rose's mom was none the wiser. She rushed to wrap Rose in a hug so strong Rose swore she felt a few ribs breaking.

"Thank you so much," Beth said. "I needed this."

Suddenly the crushing of her spine was worth it. The last week dealing with Nick's bullshit and nearly losing her job was nothing compared to the happiness of this moment. This was why Rose had left for New York in the first place, and she'd do it all over again if she had to.

When she looked over her mom's shoulder, even Vivian was smiling. It was the first time Rose had seen her genuinely happy all morning.

Yeah, this was definitely worth it.

Chapter 16

VIVIAN'S APARTMENT SAT REGALLY IN the middle of her neighborhood. It was nice for the area, clean and well laid out, and its organization matched Vivian perfectly. Rose liked it here. She could get used to visiting. The hallway in the main entrance of the complex was empty, quiet, and sanitary, and while it contained little liveliness, Rose thought silence was better than annoying neighbors.

Vivian wiped her feet on the welcome mat then fished her keys out of her pocket. From the wall of miniature mailboxes, she unlocked the one with her name on it and tucked her bills under her arm like this was an everyday occurrence, like nothing about her routine changed for her just because she was bringing Rose home with her now.

Rose browsed a few titles of flyers on the bulletin board while she waited.

No pets allowed.

Vacant rooms available for rent.

Pool hours: 10 a.m. to 9 p.m.

Rose lost herself in thoughts of skinny dipping when Vivian called to her from the first step.

"You coming?"

"Is that a euphemism?"

"If you want it to be."

She did.

Rose bounded after Vivian on the stairs, glad to discover that Vivian only lived on the second floor and that she wouldn't be forced to sweat every time she came over. If Vivian would let her, she expected to be here a lot, and Rose had no intention of tiring herself out before they even got to the sex. She should probably get acquainted with the elevator. Then again, if she had Vivian's ass to look at every time she made her way to the second floor she could deal with it.

They reached Vivian's door, and while she fumbled with her keys Rose couldn't resist and cupped the ass that had tantalized her all the way up the stairs. Vivian's head whipped around, checking to see if anyone was nearby.

"You can't wait for me to open the door?" she asked.

"Relax. No one's around. This isn't the office." Rose found her own words comforting, but she caved to Vivian's protests anyway. She slid her hands back into her pockets and made them promise to behave.

Vivian smiled in gratitude and opened the door.

The first thing that hit Rose about Vivian's apartment wasn't the smell, but the lack of it. It was the nonexistent scent of somewhere familiar, of home, and Rose wondered if she had spent so much time around Vivian that she had become desensitized to her scent.

The hallway by the door led directly into the kitchen, which was compact. A bowl of fruit rested on a counter by the coffee pot and toaster. A microwave and a couple of other appliances cluttered up the rest. The countertops may have been crowded, but the small dining room table between the kitchen and the living room was bare. At home, Rose's dining table was full of paperwork, bills, and schoolwork from both her and her mother, and just the fact that Rose could walk up to Vivian's table and find a place to set her plate down made her envious.

The living room was nearly as sparse as the kitchen, but Vivian had at least taken some time to decorate it, throwing a couple of abstract paintings around the room and picking out dark leather sofas to contrast the white walls. The TV on the wall wasn't anything impressive, but it wasn't small either, and Rose could comfortably sit through a movie night here, bundled up on the couch with Vivian at her side and a bowl of popcorn in her lap. She almost wanted to sit down now, to test the leather and see what books Vivian had on the coffee table next to her coasters, but Vivian snapped her out of her thoughts by slapping her mail on top of the fake fireplace.

"I know it's probably not up to your standards," Vivian said. "But I like to think it's nicer than our hotel room."

"It's not like I live in a mansion," Rose said. "It's nice in here. I'd like to get an apartment like this someday."

"Want to see the bedroom?" Vivian asked, and the lowered tone of her voice told Rose this wasn't part of the house tour.

Rose outstretched her hand for Vivian to take. Vivian didn't even hesitate in grasping it. "Lead the way, Ms. President."

Hand in hand, they walked to the bedroom adjacent to the living room. The room itself was medium sized, plenty big enough for one person and certainly big enough for two who were used to spending time with each other in small enclosed places like a hotel room.

The closet door was made of sliding wood panels, closed, no doubt to conceal a wardrobe of crisp, ironed business suits suspended on wire hangers beside a dresser packed tightly with pants and underwear as neatly folded into the drawers as they had been inside Vivian's suitcase. The laundry was either done or craftily concealed in a basket where Rose couldn't see it, because there certainly weren't any clothes strewn across the floor like a makeshift carpet as there had been by the end of their hotel stay. Rose preferred the cleanliness.

The bed was the most important thing, and it was nice, queen-sized, and made. The sheets looked soft and there was only one way Rose was going to find out if they were. She let go of Vivian's hand to dive onto the bed, wrinkling the covers as the pull of her weight untucked them from the corners of the mattress. She sighed, content. The bed was just as soft as it looked. But not as warm without Vivian in it with her.

Vivian watched Rose relax with a smile on her face, but Rose didn't stare back at Vivian so innocently. She smirked, pulled herself onto her elbows, and beckoned Vivian over with two fingers, curling them suggestively into the air.

As Vivian approached, Rose raised onto her knees. Vivian leaned down to capture Rose's lips, and Rose kissed her back, hands roaming over Vivian's hips before settling into her belt loops, tugging her forward until her knees hit the edge of the mattress.

The first thing to go was Vivian's shirt. One by one, Rose unclasped the pearl buttons, starting at Vivian's collar and exposing more and more of her torso until a clear line of skin trailed from Vivian's chin to her pants, only interrupted by the thin fabric strand of her bra. When her shirt was fully undone, Rose peeled away the garment from Vivian's shoulders, letting it fall to the floor at Vivian's feet before tackling her bra and sliding her hands around Vivian's back to undo the clasp.

Vivian helped her remove the fabric and allowed Rose's hands to roam back to her front, over the skin between her breasts, before cupping each mound in her palms. Nipples stiff, Vivian gasped as Rose's mouth closed around one bud, sucking diligently on the skin until it was sore. She lavished one breast thoroughly, mouth and palm working in sync to stimulate Vivian until she was forced to guide Rose to avoid oversensitivity. Tucking a fist gently into Rose's curls, she tugged Rose to her other breast, sighing with a mixture of pleasure and relief when Rose began working her other nipple, tongue flicking up and down the peak before swirling around it. When she started sucking, Vivian gasped again and pulled her away.

Rose smirked as Vivian began undoing her pants.

"Take off your shirt," Vivian ordered. "It's only fair you get the same treatment I do. Guests come first."

"In that case"—Rose threw off her sweater then moved to help Vivian slide her pants around her legs—"looks like you're the guest."

Rose wasn't slow about removing Vivian's briefs. She slid them down her thighs before Vivian had kicked her pants off her ankles, and Rose's lips met the top of her mound, kissing the skin for permission before going lower, while Vivian's briefs slid along her legs to the floor, catching up with her pants. Vivian kicked the clothes away from her before nodding, looking down to meet Rose's eye as Rose looked up at her.

Rose's tongue repeated the same motions it had on Vivian's nipple, sucking on her clit and swirling around the bud until she had Vivian whining again and leaning further into the mattress for support. When Rose's tongue traveled lower, prodding its tip into Vivian's entrance, Vivian's legs shook, thighs spasming with the novel burst of pleasure.

Vivian reached down to grip Rose's shoulders, steadying herself to take some of the weight off her legs. Rose could tell she was having a hard time keeping herself up, legs spread as far apart as possible to allow Rose room to work, and fingers digging deeper into Rose's shoulder blades the deeper Rose's tongue got lost inside her. Vivian was dripping onto her, supplying an endless amount of lubricant for Rose to use to maneuver around inside her, stroking every crevice she could reach, and it wasn't any surprise when Vivian's walls clamped down around the muscle.

Rose gripped the back of Vivian's thighs as she orgasmed, holding her in place when her legs buckled beneath her. She squeezed the flesh there gently, kneading the skin below her ass before taking the cheeks into her palms. She massaged the skin until Vivian came down, cheeks red and breath heavier than it was before. As soon as she recovered, she bent down to kiss Rose, and Rose intentionally brought her tongue into the mix, letting Vivian savor herself.

Rose got so lost in the way their mouths moved together that it startled her when Vivian pushed her over onto her side, lying Rose down before straddling her.

Hair splayed on the pillow, Rose's eyes widened as she looked up and saw Vivian smirking above her.

"Your turn," Vivian said.

Rose didn't disagree with her this time.

As soon as she realized Rose was ready to comply, Vivian

unmounted her, foregoing straddling Rose to sink all the way down her body, pulling off clothes as she went. First Rose's bra, then her pants and underwear in one go, all the way down to her socks. She tossed the growing pile of clothes to the floor with her own, then kissed her way back up Rose's body, spending time on her calves, her thighs, and her hips, and only stopping when her face hovered above Rose's sex, her breath tickling Rose's bundle of nerves.

She made eye contact with Rose and waited for her nod before lowering her mouth, taking Rose's lips between her own, and tasting the tang on them. Rose's fluids were already spilling and her clit was already swollen, and she had Vivian to thank for that. Watching Vivian cum never failed to turn her on, and it didn't help that they hadn't gotten to finish what they started earlier at the office. Rose's underwear had been ruined hours ago, and she knew it wouldn't take long for Vivian to ruin hers too.

As soon as Vivian's tongue met her clit, Rose was blissed out, only halfway conscious, as she experienced the closest thing to an out-of-body experience she probably ever would. Vivian wasn't slow in her licks, wasn't subtle in the fact that she wanted to give Rose as much pleasure as possible, and Rose was cumming before she knew what hit her, then cumming a second time before her first orgasm had really stopped. She was pretty sure the second one wasn't intentional, though—just a happy accident, the byproduct of Vivian lingering too long as she tried to clean up her mess.

When Vivian raised her head from between Rose's legs again, her mouth was glistening like a divine aura, and Rose gave her a kiss worthy of someone holy.

Vivian made herself comfortable beside Rose, shoving the extra pillow under her head for support. They kissed on their sides, facing each other as their arms wrapped around each other, hands exploring bare backs and bare hips.

Rose only spoke when the kissing turned lazy.

"I'm glad I got to see your place."

Vivian cringed. "That sounds like a good-bye."

"It's not," Rose said. "Unless you want me to go. You can tell me if I'm overextending my stay."

Vivian shook her head, wrapping her arm tighter around Rose. "You don't have to go. I'm used to spending the night with you."

Rose smiled and snuggled unconsciously into Vivian's side. It wasn't a hard decision for her to make. "I'll stay," she said, making a note to let her mother know she wouldn't be home that night. "Can we get dinner, though? I'm starving."

"Do you want to order Chinese takeout?"

"What a dumb question," Rose scolded. "I always want to order Chinese takeout."

Chapter 17

THE COFFEE SHOP ACROSS THE street from the office wasn't a far walk, but Rose couldn't help but check the clock on her phone every few seconds. As much as she wanted to savor the moment and the coffee with Phoebe, her break would only last so long.

"You seem distracted," Phoebe said. "Even more than usual. And I didn't think that was possible."

Rose set her cup down on her saucer and locked her phone. "Sorry. Just watching the time."

"Vivian got you working that hard? We've barely gotten a chance to talk to each other since you came back from New York."

She had been back in DC for a week now, but with so many excursions to Vivian's house, Rose had forgotten all about her promise to catch up with Phoebe. That's what they were supposed to be doing now. "It's not Vivian. Well." Rose paused. "It's not work, anyway."

Phoebe's face lit up as she bit into scone. "I take it things are going well?"

"Very."

"Oh, come on. You've got to give me more than that." Phoebe dusted her fingers off on a napkin. Rose came clean.

"She's great."

"If you haven't gotten tired of her yet, then clearly she is."

"What do you mean *if I haven't gotten tired of her yet*?"

"It's not like you've ever had a real relationship," Phoebe said.

"You sleep with someone and you get bored with them, or you start seeing someone and it immediately goes south."

Rose couldn't deny her less-than-perfect track record. "Well, I'm definitely not bored of her yet. I was actually scared we'd stop sleeping together once we got back to DC. That's how very much not bored of her I am."

"So you're dating?"

Rose took a sip of coffee to stall. "No." Phoebe raised an eyebrow. "We haven't talked about it. There's no need to rush."

"If you're ignoring your best friend to spend time with her, then you probably need to talk about it."

Phoebe had a point, but it still felt too soon. She and Vivian had a nice groove going. It was fun, light. There was no need to ruin a good thing by overcomplicating it.

Rose glanced at her phone again. She chugged the last of her coffee. "Speaking of ignoring you, I don't mean to, but I really have to go. I'm meeting Vivian."

"On your break?"

Rose shrugged.

"Gross." Phoebe snorted.

"Rude."

"Sorry," Phoebe said. "I shouldn't be riding your ass about it anyway. I'm glad you're sleeping with Vivian. Now that she's getting laid, she's less of a bitch."

Vivian's reputation around the office was improving lately, mostly because she was being less of a hardass. It wasn't because she was getting laid, though. Vivian had been sleeping with Jana long before Rose came along. It was the fact that the office was running smoothly and efficiently and the finances were once again in order that was relaxing Vivian. She didn't have to be as stressed or as strict when productivity was up.

Rose would take the credit for her improved mood, though. She almost wished she could attribute Vivian's rise in mood to their relationship.

Not that it was a relationship.

Yeah, Phoebe was right. She really needed to talk to Vivian about what they had.

"She'll be a bitch for the rest of the afternoon if you cock block her by stalling me." Rose stood from the table. "Now, if you'll excuse me."

As Rose walked outside, she looked at her phone clock. She had fourteen minutes until the end of her break. She was late, but not too late. She could make it to the supply closet with plenty of time to spare.

The office wasn't built for sex. The storage closets were empty and tiny, barely big enough for one person to walk into, and when Rose found herself shut inside of them with Vivian, it reminded her of watching nerds being shoved into lockers in high school. The closet had always seemed cavernous before, but now that the shelves were stocked full of stationary and all the supplies Gio Corp. DC could finally afford, suddenly, the space seemed tiny and cramped. Fitting inside the closet was a hassle, but it was a hassle very much worth the effort.

Rose tugged the string of the lightbulb dangling above their heads to let them see in the dark closet. The best sight was Vivian's work ensemble. She wore a charcoal, mid-calf pencil skirt with a white, button-up blouse that Rose had to strongly resist ripping off her, and under that, a skin tone bra a few shades lighter than Vivian's complexion. Its contours were clearly visible beneath the thin material of the blouse, and Rose wondered if Vivian had purposefully chosen the outfit just to tease her.

"You're late." Vivian's voice was a playful whisper.

"You going to fire me for my tardiness?"

"No."

Making up for lost time, Vivian was quick to pull Rose in for a hurried kiss.

Even with Gene's consent to their relationship, fooling around on the job was only going to get both of them fired. There was no funny business on the clock. It was a rule strictly enforced and put in place by Vivian, which Rose accepted and automatically followed.

On their breaks, though, they weren't technically on the clock.

To the rest of the office, Vivian intentionally came off as the kind of person who would never be caught dead making out with a subordinate in the office supply closet in the middle of the afternoon. However, Rose knew another Vivian—the Vivian that got handsy in the back of cabs, the Vivian that let Rose go down on her in the shower—and it didn't take much convincing to get this other Vivian into the supply closet with her. It wasn't either of their first choices, but they both agreed that it got the job done, and that was what was important.

Rose wrapped her arms around Vivian's waist, swaying them both slightly as they kissed. It was nice until Rose moved too much and smacked the back of her head against a shelf. She pulled her lips away from Vivian's to hiss the pain away.

"Are you all right?"

"Yeah," Rose said. She rubbed her scalp where the shelving had hit. She might have a small knot there tomorrow, but it was nothing major. No concussion. "You know, we wouldn't be having this problem if you just let me eat you out under your desk."

Vivian rolled her eyes. "Then you'd just be smacking your head against the bottom of the desk instead of the envelope shelf."

That was…probably true.

"Besides," Vivian said. "There's too many windows in my office. Someone would see, and it's not exactly professional to orgasm on the job, especially not when the person you're having sex with is one of your own employees."

"Come on, you and Jana never fooled around in the office?" Rose asked, genuinely curious. She wrapped her arms around Vivian's midriff and pushed their bodies closer together.

"We kept things to our apartments."

"Why fuck me in the storage closet then?" Rose asked. "Why not make me wait till after work and take me home like you did with her?"

"You're harder to resist." Vivian tilted her head and nibbled lightly at Rose's neck. Rose threaded her hands into Vivian's hair to encourage her. That was a good enough explanation for Rose. They were running out of time. If they wanted to make the most of their break, they had to get moving, fast.

Vivian's hands were impatient on Rose's hips, fingers wedging themselves inside where Rose's blouse tucked into her pants. She loosened the fabric from its tuck before undoing the button on Rose's trousers and sliding her hands delicately along the hem, fingers tracing a line of goose bumps into Rose's skin. Rose's shudder was more than enough consent for Vivian to dip her fingers beneath the fabric, running her fingertips over the top of Rose's mound teasingly.

Rose kissed Vivian fervently, teeth accidentally and then not so accidentally scraping Vivian's lower lip as Vivian's fingers scraped her pubes, ruffling the small patch of hair with delicate circles. Rose was breathing heavily with anticipation, and when Vivian finally wedged her hand further down Rose's underwear, Rose braced herself against the wall, laying her back flat along the cool concrete surface as Vivian's fingers probed her warmth, two fingers scissoring her lips apart before starting a circular rhythm on her clit, rubbing around each side of Rose's bud.

Rose had been waiting all morning for this, and consequently she had already worked herself up. She wasn't dry when Vivian caressed her, and the satisfaction of someone finally taking care of the ache she'd cursed herself with made it very difficult for her not to moan. The supply closet wasn't out of the way enough for that, though, and Rose was forced to find another way to quiet herself.

To distract herself from becoming overwhelmed with the pleasure, Rose's hands matched Vivian's, tugging on the button of her pants until it was free and she could slip a hand beneath the band of her underwear. Her fingers dove for Vivian's clit straight away, pulsing at the wetness and feeling Vivian adjust her stance to allow Rose more room to stroke her, fingers gliding up and down her slit with ease.

Hearing Vivian keen into her ear was doing wonders for Rose. Her noises were escalating, whimpers higher and higher pitched, and Rose finally caved in and kissed her just to shut the both of them up.

Rose heard the jostling of the doorknob before she heard the footsteps outside the door.

She split herself apart from Vivian immediately, tugging the hand out of her pants and pulling down her shirt to cover up the fact that her dress pants were unbuttoned. Vivian scrambled backward, wiping the lipstick off her mouth with the back of her hand.

Of all the people who might barge in on them, of course it was Rose's mom.

Rose was more than aware that her hair was a mess and that her shirt was skewed at the collar, but she could do nothing but subtly try to rearrange herself as Beth eyed both of them suspiciously. Rose ran her fingers through her hair as Vivian turned around and pretended to search for something important on the shelf behind her. Beth shifted awkwardly by the door, probably because there wasn't enough room for her to fully step in.

"Sorry, I didn't know anyone was in here." Her tone implied that she knew she was interrupting something, Rose just prayed she didn't know what.

"Uh, Mom, hey. Did you need something?" Rose asked the question like she was the supply closet assistant, ready to help her fellow employees find whatever they needed. That didn't explain what she was doing in here, though. Vivian was doing a good job of rummaging around for some imaginary item and avoiding Beth's gaze.

"Staples," Beth said.

"That's what we're looking for, too." Rose had crafted better lies, but it was the best she could think of in the heat of the moment. "We can't find them. We think somebody's already used them all."

Vivian finally turned around, vehemently nodding in agreement with Rose.

"They're right there." Beth pointed to a spot just beside Rose's head.

Sure enough, when Rose turned around the staples were right in front of her face. "Well, that explains why we couldn't find them over there." She laughed then grabbed the box and handed it to her mother, fully expecting her to leave now that she had what she wanted, only Beth didn't move.

Beth gestured to the box. "Did you need some of these?"

"You know what," Rose said. "There's probably another box. We'll find it. You can have those."

Beth was quiet for a moment, then chose to abandon whatever thought she was having. "All right. Thanks." Beth was quick to get out of there, probably because the longer the three of them stood in the room, the more claustrophobic it became. Rose could barely breathe. It helped that her mom left the door open, and Rose hoped that was a sign that she didn't know why it had been shut in the first place.

Vivian was quick to correct that error. She shut the door as soon as Beth's footsteps couldn't be heard down the hallway. Sighing, she rested her back against the frame and stared at Rose from across the room, no more than a couple of feet separating them.

"Do you think she saw anything?" Rose asked.

"I don't know," Vivian said. "I don't think so. If she did, she'd have said something."

"Then we're good," Rose said. She took a deep breath and strode over toward Vivian. Her footsteps were slow and deliberate. Her body pinned Vivian even more securely against the door, leaving her with less room to move than before. "How much time do we have left?" she asked.

Vivian glanced at her watch. "Three minutes. We don't have time."

"I've definitely made you cum faster than that," Rose said.

"I don't want to risk it," Vivian said. "If we don't finish in time I don't think I'll survive being that worked up in my office for the rest of the afternoon."

"I'm already worked up." Rose could feel the wetness smear between her thighs every time her legs shifted. "You could probably take care of me in less than three minutes."

"I have a better idea," Vivian said. "I'll make it up to you with a trip. Maybe we could go somewhere sometime?"

Rose didn't have plans this weekend. Spending a Saturday with Vivian sounded heavenly. "Where did you have in mind?"

"I promised I'd take you sightseeing, didn't I? I'm a woman of my word."

"Where are we going to go?"

"It's a surprise. I don't want to tell you yet."

"Sounds like you haven't thought of anywhere yet," Rose said.

Vivian blushed. Rose kissed her cheek until the redness faded away.

"Is it that obvious? I do have a couple places in mind. I just want to make sure I have a plan."

"And if we go somewhere I've already been?"

"Then it will still be your first time going there with me."

Rose couldn't ignore the flip of her stomach. Vivian was right. She had just opened up a whole new world to Rose. Everywhere would be new to her now. Every experience was one completely different than the ones she'd had before Vivian came into her life. She could go anywhere with Vivian by those standards.

"I can't wait."

Chapter 18

ROSE STARED AT THE BUILDING before her. "We're going ice skating?"

"Yes. That's okay, isn't it? If you hate it, I figured we could just go inside the museum," Vivian said.

The National Gallery of Art was a museum with a sculpture garden and ice rink outside of it. The place was a beautiful oasis of culture, and Rose almost always made yearly trips to visit in the winter time. She was giddy just at the prospect of being here with Vivian.

"Yeah, that's totally okay. I love the National Gallery. Me and my mom go ice skating all the time."

"I haven't been ice skating ever," Vivian said. A nervous edge sliced her voice.

"Don't worry. It's easy."

The subject was quickly dropped. From the parking lot they made their way inside the building, and Vivian paid for their admission just as she had paid for their cabs and the food they had ordered in last night. She was quiet, though. When she spoke, her voice was nervous. "What size shoe do you wear?"

Rose eased the tension by making a joke. "Do you have a foot fetish we need to talk about?"

"We need to rent skates, Rose."

Rose knew that. It wasn't like she hadn't done this before. "Six," she told the girl behind the counter. She presented the boots with a smile, though Rose was less than excited to take them from her. "Which is a lot fewer than the number of people who have worn these skates before me. Yuck."

"I'm trying not to think about it." Vivian handed her money over in exchange for both of their rentals. The skates didn't smell too badly, much to Rose's surprise, but it was cold and her nose was numb. She could barely smell anything. "At least renting ice skates is classier than renting bowling shoes," Vivian said.

Rose shuddered. "Thank you for not taking me bowling."

"You're welcome. I'm good at bowling, though."

"Of course you would be. Bowling is the most boring sport. It's not even a sport."

Vivian frowned as she tugged her boots on. She busied her hands with tying her laces. "They air games on ESPN."

"You watch ESPN?" Rose asked as she tied her own laces.

"No, but Jana liked it. She preferred pool, though. Lots of lesbians smacking around a bunch of balls. She's into it."

"I'm more into cute ice skaters, especially when they get lifted in the air and you can see up their skirts."

"I'm afraid I may not be that graceful," Vivian said. "I'm also not wearing a skirt." They were both bundled up, wearing thick jackets and scarves. Rose appreciated how the ice skaters on TV managed to show so much skin without freezing to death.

"I'm sure you'll do fine."

Vivian did not do fine.

"You look like a giraffe on roller blades." Rose laughed.

Vivian gripped the railings like she was hanging on to the edge of a cliff. She kind of was. If she fell one more time, there was a good chance it might be the time the blades of the skates lodged themselves into her leg or her ass, which would not be pretty. Rose was going to let her use the railing as much as she needed. She skated freely beside Vivian, staying close in case Vivian needed her help.

"This was an awful idea." Vivian's voice wavered more than her

178

legs. Her face was pale, and Rose couldn't tell if it was because of the cold or her nerves.

"This is actually a lot of fun," Rose said. "For me, anyway."

"I'm glad one of us is having a good time." Her tone was only half bitter.

"Come on, you'll get the hang of it. It just takes a bit of practice. Here." Rose extended her hand and offered it to Vivian who looked at it like she didn't trust it. Her hands stayed glued to the railings.

"I don't want to take you down with me," she said.

"You'll never get anywhere on the railings." Rose kept her hand outstretched. "If we both fall I won't be mad. I promise we won't, though. I'll keep you steady."

Vivian looked from Rose's eyes to her hand again, hesitant, but after a moment of contemplation she pried one of her hands from the railing and laced her pale fingers in Rose's gloved ones. They shuffled their feet along for a few yards, hand in hand, Rose skating and Vivian trying to walk along in her boots until Rose got fed up with the choppiness of their pace.

"You have to move your feet properly," Rose said. "I promise we'll go slow."

"You sure?"

Rose nodded. Vivian kept her arms outstretched for a moment like a tightrope walker as she balanced herself while Rose kept her upright.

"There you go. You're getting the hang of it."

She wasn't, really. They were still moving at two inches an hour, but Rose didn't mind. The rest of the rink skated around her in a blur. The other skaters were background noise as she focused on Vivian and the intense look of concentration on her face

She could have stayed in their own little world forever if someone hadn't clipped her arm, almost knocking both her and Vivian down in the process.

"Move faster, Grandma!"

Rose recognized the voice immediately.

"Phoebe!"

Phoebe stopped dead in her tracks ahead of them before spinning around to face them. The brunette beside her stopped, too, and it took all of two seconds for Rose to realize Phoebe and Harley were here on a date.

It also took all of two seconds for Phoebe to realize who she had just insulted.

"Vivian! Oh my God, I'm so sorry. I swear, that wasn't an insult. I love my grandma! Not that I love you or anything, but…"

Vivian's eyes were angry, but dulled slightly with fear, too, and she kept quiet as she regained her stance. One arm reached out for the railing again, but her other hand held onto Rose. Her glance darted between Harley and Phoebe knowingly.

Rose butted in before Vivian could say anything, either about Harley and Phoebe clearly being here as a couple or Phoebe's rudeness. "What are you guys doing here?" she asked.

"Just…chilling," Harley said, eyeing Vivian as suspiciously as Vivian was eyeing her.

"Well, we're gonna go," Phoebe said. "We'll leave you two alone. It was nice seeing you outside of work, Vivian. Sorry about the whole bumping into you guys thing."

"It was nice to see you, too," Vivian said. She was all professionalism.

Harley smiled at her, looking as awkward as Vivian. Then she reached down to tug on Phoebe's hand, pulling her away as fast as possible. Off they skated, leaving at high speed.

"That was embarrassing," Vivian said after they had gone.

"Are you embarrassed because they saw us together or because they saw you trying to skate?"

"I didn't know you told them about us."

"It's okay," Rose said. "They're not going to say anything. If they haven't done it by now they're not going to. Plus, we have Gene's consent, so no worries."

Vivian was quiet for a moment, sawing her skates back and forth on the ice. "Why'd you tell them?" she asked. Her words were more curious than accusatory.

Rose shrugged. "Phoebe's my best friend. I talk to her about all the things that make me happy."

"I make you happy?" Vivian asked.

"If I wasn't having a good time with you, do you really think I'd be here right now?"

Vivian fell quiet again, but her smile had returned. She nursed it slowly as she stared down at her feet. "Do you want to get out of here? I've had enough skating for the rest of the year. And the rest of my life."

Rose laughed and hooked her arm around Vivian's, letting their hands unclasp. "Yes, we can go. I want to see the sculptures, anyway."

Rose offered to help Vivian skate her way back to the exit ramp of the rink, but Vivian still didn't trust that she wouldn't knock both of them down. She stuck to the railings, two hands on the metal, with Rose's arm wrapped around her. Rose's phone buzzed in her pocket before they were even off the ice.

It was a message from Phoebe.

"I knew you were sleeping with Vivian, but you didn't tell me you were already going on romantic dates."

"It's not a date."

Rose typed back one-handed, tilting her phone away from Vivian's sight line, although she was too busy concentrating on her feet to snoop over Rose's shoulder.

Phoebe's reply came faster than Rose's.

"Right. I hold hands with all of my friends when we go ice skating, too."

"She needed help."

Rose answered.

"Uh-huh. Whatever you say."

Rose put her phone back in her pocket without responding. She didn't have time to explain everything to Phoebe, and she also had to help Vivian off the ice. When she stepped onto solid ground, Vivian looked like a fish thrown back into the water. Her relief was palpable.

She was super quick to take off her skates and even quicker to exchange them for her shoes. Rose's own feet were happy to be back inside something that both fit her and actually belonged to her, and she was fairly excited by the prospect of going home and washing the smell of someone else's feet off her.

The National Gallery of Art's sculpture garden was an installation surrounding the building. Sculptures from some of the greats—Roy Lichtenstein, Claes Oldenburg—surrounded the museum, and Rose couldn't believe that such masterpieces were left out in the elements and not shielded within the walls of the museum itself. The only thing more beautiful was Vivian, whom Rose hadn't let go of since they'd left the skating rink. They walked arm in arm toward the garden, nearly stepping on each other's toes.

"I can walk on my own now, you know?"

"I know."

"You're still holding me."

"What, are you shy?"

Vivian's cheeks reddened, but Rose couldn't be sure if it was a blush or the cold.

The sculptures were stationed in the garden year round, but they were by far the most beautiful in winter. Most of the snow had been cleared away so the pieces became splashes of color among a snow-white background. Every time she visited, Rose had a new favorite piece. They took their time and looked at all of them, despite the cold, as they made their way back to the parking lot.

"I like this one," Vivian said, pointing out the sculpture closest to the parking lot. It was a Robert Indiana piece, four letters stacked together reading, *AMOR*.

"Reminds me of Harley and Phoebe," Rose said. "They're a cute couple."

"They are."

"I get totally jealous when I see them together. Don't tell Phoebe that, but I want a relationship like theirs someday." Rose was silent for a moment, weighing the words on her mind. "I think I could have it with you."

The reflection of the snow sparkled in Vivian's eyes. It was the only explanation for the light Rose saw in them.

Rose gnawed at her bottom lip. "I like you. I think I could even love you. But I also think we should take it slow. We have something good, and I don't want to ruin it. I'm going back to college soon. You just got out of that fiasco with Jana. I don't want us to end up like that, rushing into things, but then again, I don't want us rushing out of them either." Rose released Vivian's arm and stuffed her hands in her pockets.

"I'm partway through my final year," she continued. "And if I take the internship Gene offered me, and I'd be mad not to, we could end up spending a lot of time together. It wouldn't be a fling, it wouldn't be temporary, and I don't want it to be awkward either. I want to do this the right way. But only if you want it, too."

The twinkle in Vivian's eye wasn't the snow anymore. Not even the sun itself shone that brightly. She took Rose's hand.

"I like you, Rose. I like you a lot."

Rose wrapped her arms around Vivian's neck, tucked her face into the crook of her shoulder. Vivian's skin was so warm, and smelled so nice, of spice and lotion and the bath soaps Rose had bought her, that she didn't ever want to separate, didn't ever want the hug to end.

"So do you want to try this? Officially?" she asked.

If Vivian could get any softer, she did. Her skin melted against Rose's, and Rose's insides melted along with her. Vivian wrapped her arms around her and squeezed Rose like she'd never let her go. "Yes," she whispered. "I'd like to try—very, very much."

A sense of calm washed over Rose. Even when Vivian pulled away from the hug, she still felt at peace.

"Let's go back to my place," Vivian said. "It's freezing out here."

Rose had no qualms with that. Phoebe might have chastised her for the time she spent with Vivian, but now Rose felt no guilt about spending another night at her girlfriend's apartment.

With one hand in Vivian's, she fished her phone out of her jacket with the other. She sent one quick text to Phoebe before pocketing the phone for good.

"Okay, we might be dating."

Epilogue

ROSE KICKED THAT ACCOUNTING EXAM'S ass so hard the school was going to have to suspend her for violence on campus. Normally, after doing that well on an exam, she would reward herself with a lazy week, maybe skip a few classes or put off a couple of trivial homework assignments, but she couldn't do that anymore. She was done with school. Forever. This was her last exam. Graduation was only a week away, and yet standing on stage and accepting that diploma wasn't the most exciting thing happening to her this week.

As the rest of the students filed out of the classroom and toward the exit of the building, Rose stayed behind. She found a quiet corner, and back against the wall, pressed her phone to her ear.

It rang only once before Vivian picked up. "Hey, how'd it go?"

"Wow, I don't even get a 'hi?'"

Vivian huffed on the other end of the line. "Hi, Rose."

"How do you think it went?" Rose asked.

"Knowing you, either you aced it or you missed the exam entirely because there was a line at Starbucks and you refused to go to class without your coffee."

"Well, you're looking at a woman with both a degree and a completed punch card worth one free latte next time I visit."

"I knew you could manage both. Congratulations! But I'm not looking at you at all, Rose. We're on the phone."

"Well, you will be seeing me soon. And a lot more often. I'm coming over tomorrow."

"Come over now. We should celebrate."

The crowd in the hall had quickly dissipated. A few stragglers were all that was left behind. Rose waved to a few familiar smiling faces.

"As much as I would love that, you know I have to go home and pack up my last few things. Moving out doesn't happen overnight."

"And it's not every day that you graduate college and earn your degree," Vivian said in return. "Come over. You've got plenty of stuff at my place for the night."

"Or I can get packing out of the way tonight and then spend all day with you tomorrow." Usually, Vivian was the more practical of the two of them. Begging Rose to abandon her responsibilities was uncharacteristic of her, even if part of Rose did welcome it and was eager to throw caution to the wind for the night. She was a woman with a degree now, though. She had to have a bit of pragmatism to show for it.

"Please come over," Vivian said. "I'll make it worth your while."

"Does that mean sex?"

A girl across the hallway in the commons area looked up at her in shocked disgust, glared, then went back to reading the textbook in her lap. Rose blushed in embarrassment and tried to hold back a laugh.

"If that's what it takes to get you to come over, sure."

"Okay, I'll come, but Phoebe is taking me out for drinks later, so I can't stay."

"That's fine," Vivian said. "I'll see you in a bit."

"See you."

Rose hung up and wandered down the hall. She was in no rush to go back to Vivian's apartment, and being alone in the empty hallway of her campus's business building made her nostalgic. She had spent four years studying here, and now she was probably never going to see the inside of this building again. She scanned the decorations on the walls. Faculty pictures. Department accomplishments. Flyers for school events. A row of alumni portraits caught her eye. They were all old students who had gone on to do something great. They were CEOs of companies, owners of small, local businesses, owners of national chains Rose recognized. Maybe she would be back in this building someday. Maybe she'd be on this wall.

She took the bus from campus downtown to Vivian's apartment, flashing her student ID to the driver as payment for the last time. Rose wouldn't miss the classes, but she would miss the student benefits.

Vivian's apartment was all too familiar to her now. She could no longer count the number of times she'd visited nor the number of nights she'd stayed over on weekends between classes. Rose's first time visiting after their trip to New York seemed like a lifetime ago. It practically was. She entered the front door of the complex with a swipe of Vivian's spare key card and scaled the stairs with comfortable familiarity.

Something was off, though. Vivian's door was open.

As friendly as Vivian was once she let her walls down, she wasn't one to leave her physical defenses unguarded, especially to strangers in a semi-public space. The two of them knew the neighbors only through noise complaints and mixed-up mail, and that didn't constitute an open door policy to their community. Rose approached the inside of the apartment carefully, prepared for anything that might pop out at her.

"Surprise!"

She was not prepared for that. Out of nowhere, her mom jumped into the front hallway, followed by Vivian and then Phoebe. Rose had a miniature heart attack and nearly stumbled onto the floor in shock. Far too late she noticed the streamers hanging from the ceiling; baby pink letters spelled out, "Congratulations."

"Jesus Christ, you could have killed me!" She clutched her chest.

Beth threw a comforting hand on Rose's shoulder and giggled. "Sorry, honey. We didn't mean to scare you—too much."

Over her mother's shoulder, Rose had a better view into the living room behind her. Vivian's typically spacious, spotless living room was now packed full of boxes, boxes that very much resembled the ones Rose had packed up over the last week. She stepped into the living room to confirm her suspicions. "You guys brought all my stuff over?"

"Spent all day moving it," Phoebe said. "Took all three of us to have enough car space and arm strength to get everything up here. Why do you have so much junk?"

This was great. Rose had spent all week loathing the idea of carting her entire life in boxes across town. The three of them could not have chosen a better way to surprise her. "I knew I liked you guys for a reason." Then she spotted the coffee table, cluttered with different chips and dipping sauces and a six pack of beer and somehow Rose loved them even more. "You threw me a party?"

"Well," Phoebe said. "As much of a party as four people can be."

"I bought a cake, too," Vivian said.

Rose was taken aback. She hadn't expected this. She knew her mom was proud of her, that Vivian was happy for her, and that Phoebe wanted to celebrate her accomplishments, but she didn't expect the three of them to come together to pull this off for her. "I don't know what to say."

"Don't say anything. It's your graduation present! It's the least we could do." Phoebe wrapped Rose in a hug that she was quick to return.

"Does this mean we aren't going out for drinks later?" Rose asked.

"No. This is the drinks." Phoebe held up the six pack of beer. "You should celebrate with Vivian tonight. This was her idea, you know? You and I can go out any old time."

Vivian stood sheepishly off to the side, apparently embarrassed to be outed as the mastermind behind this surprise. Rose found it endearing.

"What kind of cake did you get me?"

Vivian led her into the kitchen. Rose could still hear her mom and Phoebe in the living room sliding boxes across the hardwood floors and trying to help unpack, but it was nice to sneak a quiet moment away with Vivian.

On the counter was a simple chocolate sheet cake with the words "Congrats, Grad!" sprawled across the sponge in blood red icing. "God, I love chocolate." Rose scraped a finger along the edge of the cake, capturing a nice dollop of frosting that she licked away. She moaned. "This is the best present."

Vivian wrapped her arms around Rose's waist. "Even better than getting to move in with me?"

"It's a tie," Rose said.

Vivian laughed.

"Did you really take the entire day off just to buy me a cake and help me move in?"

Vivian nodded. "Don't thank me. Thank Bailey. He's the best vice president I've ever had. He runs the place almost smoother than I do. You should see him at work. The man was born for management."

Rose would see him soon enough. As soon as she had that degree in hand, she was taking Gene up on his offer of a new position at Gio Corp. DC. If someone had told Rose last year that she'd not only still be working with Gio but actually wanting to work there, she would have called them crazy. But things were so different now. A year ago, Gio had been a dump that did nothing but suck the life out of her and her friends, and Rose had helped change that with her own two hands. Now the DC branch of Gio Corp. was thriving, and it didn't only employ her friends anymore. The office also provided for her mom, who had taken so easily to data entry and the office as a whole that she'd been quickly promoted to a secretarial position. It also supported Vivian, and if Vivian wasn't the most important person in Rose's life right now, she didn't know who was. She leaned in and gave Vivian a chaste kiss on the lips. A fleck of red frosting stayed behind when she pulled away.

"I think I was born for management, too," Rose said. "You better watch out. Someday Gene might give me your job."

Vivian let out something between a scoff and a laugh. "Don't even try. I know where you live, remember?"

Beth's voice called out from the living room and ruined the moment. "Rose, what's in this?"

Rose was forced to investigate. In the living room she found Beth holding one of the lighter boxes Rose had packed the night before. "This is the only one that says fragile. I don't want to break anything."

Rose recognized the box immediately. She had purposely mislabeled it to prevent snooping, and yet here Beth was. In it were her delicates, some old legal papers and a few items of revealing lingerie. And the dildo. Definitely the dildo.

"Mom, remember that talk we had about not opening my packages?"

Beth gently set the box on the coffee table then threw her hands up in defeat. "I don't want to know."

Phoebe looked curiously at the box. "I do." She reached to open the lid, but Rose smacked her hand away playfully.

"Help me with the rest of this stuff."

It was a miracle when she did so without complaint.

Cake. Chips. A few streamers. Rose's best friend, her girlfriend, and her mom. Maybe this wasn't the liveliest party in the world, but it was enough for Rose. Her life had changed forever last year when she went to that god-awful Christmas party at Gio Corp., and here with Vivian holding her hand as they ate chips and salsa and unpacked Rose's life to move it into Vivian's own, Rose couldn't be happier. She was ready for the next big step.

By the time the evening was over, Rose was exhausted, but in a good way. Most of her things were put away, and most of her empty boxes were in the recycling bin out back. Phoebe and Beth had left her with best wishes for the first night officially living in her new apartment as well as more guacamole than she knew what to do with. Rose was looking forward to the taco party she'd have to throw this weekend almost as much as spending the rest of the night sprawling on the couch with Vivian.

The move had unearthed Rose's DVD collection. It was a small library of mostly rom coms and guilty pleasure Disney films that she was happy to add to Vivian's own DVD stash in the entertainment center. She chose an old comedy she hadn't seen in a while, popped it into the DVD player, and relaxed into Vivian's side on the couch. With a beer on the coaster in front of her, her girlfriend cuddled up to her, and an old quilt curled over both of them, Rose was in heaven. She relished the quiet peacefulness of the moment.

"Tonight was fantastic," Rose said. "Thank you for helping me move in. I couldn't have done it all by myself."

"Don't thank me," Vivian said. "Phoebe and your mom did as much of the heavy lifting as I did. They're the ones who knew what you'd want to take from home and bring over here."

"They're pretty great, aren't they?"

Vivian planted a kiss on the top of Rose's head. "Almost as great as you."

Rose hummed in contentment. The lights were dimmed, and she watched the colors of the television flicker across their hands, locked together on Vivian's lap. Vivian looked beautiful in the dark with what little light there was painting shadows across her face and highlighting the curve of her jawline.

Vivian turned her attention back to the screen for a few moments but quickly caught Rose staring at her. "Is the movie not entertaining enough?" she asked. "I knew we should have done something better than a movie night to celebrate your graduation."

"No, this is perfect," Rose said, and she meant it.

"You wouldn't rather have gone to a real party?"

"A girl in my Economics class snorted a line of cocaine off her desk yesterday after her last test. I'm not so sure the whole graduation-party life is my scene. I'd be happy to watch movies with you on the couch every night."

Vivian chuckled. "Well, you brought the entire Harry Potter octalogy, so we're good for at least the next week."

"Sign me up."

"Seriously?" Vivian asked. "You went from wanting first class flights and penthouse suites to being satisfied with a few stay-at-home movie nights?"

"I've always liked stay-at-home movie nights," Rose said. "And I still like first class flights." Rose adjusted her arm into a more comfortable position, wrapping it around the back of the couch over Vivian's shoulder. "But I like you more. We could live in a dumpster, and I'd still like you."

"I appreciate that."

Rose chuckled, thinking the comment was sarcastic.

"No, I mean it," Vivian said. "Thank you for moving in with me. When I asked you if you wanted to, I wasn't sure you would."

"Why wouldn't I? We've basically been living together since New York."

Vivian paused a moment to reminisce. If Rose stared into her eyes deep enough, she was convinced she'd see a film reel of their lives together playing out on the black screen of her pupils, starting at that Christmas party and ending right here on Vivian's couch. Their couch. "God, we have, haven't we? We spent a week living together before we were dating. Damn, that's gay."

Rose let out a hearty guffaw. "That sounds about right. How lesbian of us. The only difference now is that it's official."

"And that you brought your movie collection," Vivian said. "And a desktop so big I'm not sure we'll find a place for it in the living room."

"Hey, if you don't have a good desktop, you don't have anything. I'm surprised my mom managed to carry it all the way up here, though."

"She's a trooper," Vivian said. "She's great. I like her a lot."

"That's good because she'll probably want to visit all the time now. Sorry."

"No, don't be. I like your family. I like being a part of it."

"I think my mom likes you, too. Apart from being her boss and someone who is dating her only child, she's very uncritical of you."

Vivian smiled. "I guess it was meant to be." She toyed with Rose's fingers in her lap. The movie was long-forgotten by this point. Rose couldn't remember which one she'd picked out. "I promise we'll do something more special this weekend. We can lie on the couch and watch movies any time."

Rose cupped Vivian's cheek and stroked soothingly along her jaw line, watching the light of the television morph around her own hand now. Vivian leaned into the touch. "You're more than special enough." Rose's thumb grazed Vivian's bottom lip, caressing her gently. Vivian planted a feather-light kiss on the pad of her finger.

"I love you," Vivian said, and Rose could feel every subtle movement of her lips and every vibration of her voice as she spoke. It was the most tangible the words could ever feel, the only way she could ever physically hold them, and yet, she didn't need to. She could already feel those words, had felt them since New York. Vivian didn't have to vocalize her love for it to be true.

"I love you, too."

About Shaya Crabtree

Shaya Crabtree was born and raised in the Midwestern United States, where she studied English and Creative Writing at university. At age twelve, she began writing and never looked back long enough to put down the pencil. She prefers writing to reading and has an affinity for cryptozoology, conspiracy theories, and cooking competitions.

Other Books from Ylva Publishing

www.ylva-publishing.com

Scissor Link

Georgette Kaplan

ISBN: 978-3-95533-678-3
Length: 197 pages (72,000 words)

Wendy is in love with Janet Lace. Janet is beautiful, she's intelligent, and she is also Wendy's boss.

Still, a little fantasy never hurt anyone. Or so Wendy thought until Janet got a look at the e-mail she sent. The one about exactly what Wendy would like to do to Janet.

But when Wendy gets called into the boss's office, it might just be her fantasy coming true. If it doesn't get her fired first.

Popcorn Love

KL Hughes

ISBN: 978-3-95533-265-5
Length: Length: 347 pages (113,000 words)

Her love life lacking, wealthy fashion exec Elena Vega agrees to a string of blind dates set up by her best friend Vivian in exchange for Vivian finding a suitable babysitter for her son, Lucas. Free-spirited college student Allison Sawyer fits the bill perfectly.

Welcome to the Wallops
(The Wallops Series — Book 1)

Gill McKnight

ISBN: 978-3-95533-559-5
Length: 242 pages (67,000 words)

Jane Swallow has always struggled to keep peace, friendship, and equanimity within the community she loves, but this year everything is wrong. Her father has just been released from prison and is on his way to Lesser Wallop with the rest of her travelling family. Her job is on the line, and her ex-girlfriend has just moved in next door. Only a miracle can save her.

Just My Luck

Andrea Bramhall

ISBN: 978-3-95533-702-5
Length: 306 pages (80,500 words)

Genna Collins works a dead end job, loves her family, her girlfriend, and her friends. When she wins the biggest Euromillions jackpot on record, everything changes…and not always for the best. What if money really can't buy you happiness?

Coming from Ylva Publishing

www.ylva-publishing.com

Falling Hard

Jae

Dr. Jordan Williams devotes her life to saving patients in the OR and pleasuring women in the bedroom.

Jordan's new neighbor, single mom Emma, is the polar opposite. Family and fidelity mean everything to her.

When Emma helps Jordan recover after a bad fall, they quickly grow closer.

But neither counted on falling hard—for each other.

Wendy of the Wallops
(The Wallops Series – Book 2)

Gill McKnight

Community police officer Wendy Goodall is up to her neck in it. Sexy DI Diya Patel has seconded her to witness protection. She has a mad crush on the reclusive Dr. Lea James, and deep suspicions about wily Girl Guide leader, Kiera Minsk.

You're Fired
© 2017 by Shaya Crabtree

ISBN: 978-3-95533-754-4

Also available as e-book.

Published by Ylva Publishing, legal entity of Ylva Verlag, e.Kfr.
Ylva Verlag, e.Kfr.
Owner: Astrid Ohletz
Am Kirschgarten 2
65830 Kriftel
Germany

www.ylva-publishing.com

First edition: 2017

Credits
Edited by Gill McKnight & Robin J Samuels
Proofread by CK King
Cover Design & Print Layout by Streetlight Graphics

Printed by
booksfactory
PRINT GROUP Sp. z o.o.
ul. Ks. Witolda 7-9
71-063 Szczecin
Poland
tel./fax 91 812-43-49
NIP/USt-IdNr.: PL8522520116